PRAISE

What can I say except I absolutely loved this story, I laughed out loud and I shed emotional tears." – Amazon Reviewer (Lawfully Gifted)

"This series has quickly become one my favorites. Love the storyline, love the characters, love the back stories and love the sweet romance between each couple." – Amazon Reviewer (Remember Love)

"What an amazing start to a new series, Healing Hearts, a clean contemporary and extremely emotional tale. I loved the characters, the angst, and the honest discussions, along with the chemistry and interactions. The people are broken, but with encouragement, friendship, and the added benefit of animals, it is the beginnings for healing." – Amazon Reviewer (Remember Hope)

REMEMBER JOY

HEALING HEARTS

GINNY STERLING

INTRODUCTION

Cora Dillion thrives on control. After being abandoned and homeless on the streets, it had taken everything in her to climb back to a life she recognized. A self-proclaimed workaholic, she remains focused to prevent anyone from disrupting the existence she's built for herself. When she receives a flurry of emails from a soldier, she realizes that the man pouring out his soul could be dangerous to her structured world... and her heart.

Mike Cooper lived for the moment. Reckless and arrogant- that was the image he presented to his buddies in the barracks. Deep down inside, he needed a friend to keep him focused and was desperately afraid of the nightmarish world he existed in. Envious of the relationships around him, Mike puts his very heart on the line hoping that Cora will be the one to snatch it up.

Will Cora realize that Mike could be the very man she needs to come out of her shell? Can both of their hearts find strength in each other's weaknesses? Will the spirit of the season remind them both how to remember joy?

Each book is a stand alone story in the series. You can meet other characters, read their stories, and fall in love with them in any order.

CHAPTER 1

*J*une 2015
Ghazni, Afghanistan

MIKE COULD SEE his CPO standing near the table under the tent awning. The man was hard on them all but there was a sense of control that commanded respect to Griffin. No one ever questioned him or talked back – until Mike had arrived. He'd always been the smart-aleck in high-school and not much had changed in the last six years that he'd been in the military other than hopping from base to base. Unfortunately, this landed him smack in the middle of Afghanistan. He loved serving his country but truly hated it here. It was so foreign and so far from home that he felt isolated even when surrounded by other men in his group.

They were planning to head into the hills tomorrow to sweep for more mines. There had been an insurgence last week and several threats against them, making the whole team extremely antsy. It was times like these that made him think about his future and what he was going to do with it. When he'd signed up and took his ASVAB test, they'd joked in the office about the *goofball kid being the newest grunt in the military*. He'd scored so high that his choices were to go into the nuclear field or to go into explosives.

He chose explosives in a heartbeat – and Mike was still that goofball kid at heart, but was surrounded by a bunch of men that acted older than their ages. He was one of the youngest in their group and felt like he didn't quite fit in.

"Griffin! When you finish, they need you in berthing," Mike announced, his head peeking in the tent, interrupting several other officers that were talking nearby.

"Is it an emergency?"

"Nawww, but me and the guys –"

"Then you need to wait, like I've told you before," Griffin snapped and turned back to the map. Mike knew from the past few outings that there were caves and trails throughout the hills that were being used for munitions and hiding.

"Here and here, so we don't get pinned down," Griffin suggested, pointing at the ridge just off to the left of the map. "We can sweep West to East and hold it with far less resistance or chance of casualties. If we go in here, there are too many civilians close by. I don't want to risk my men nor anyone else. Go on, Cooper – I'll be back shortly."

That is what endeared him to Mike – the fact that this crusty older man seriously watched out for them and considered them family... even if Mike felt like the red-headed stepchild of the group.

A while later, Mike's CPO walked into the tent and glared at them. The rest of the team had received some letters a few months ago but apparently Griffin hit the jackpot. Whoever had written him had continued to write, sending box after box of treats. From what he'd heard, Griffin had a box of twinkies sent to him in the mail and Mike thought that was great.

No one ever expected the Hostess inquisition, he thought wryly as he eyed the box sitting on Griffin's immaculate bunk. It looked like the man practically ironed his sheets. The CPO seriously put them all to shame on how a soldier should behave and made them strive harder to be like him. He could have had officers' quarters but declined saying that *'loyalty made a man watch your back for you when no one else could'*.

Griffin ate, slept, and talked with them on a daily basis.

"What?" Griffin barked at them. "C'mon Radar," he called, whistling and patting his leg to call his K-9 dog to his side. Radar fell in line like clockwork. "Why can't more people be like you? You don't question, you don't talk back," he muttered, ruffling the dog's head affectionately as he strode towards his bunk space.

"Deodorant *is* a necessity, boys - Use it. It's too hot here for you *'ladies'* to go without," Griffin muttered, letting the door drop behind him. In this tent, they were equals and brothers. Mike and several others began to jeer the older man playfully. Jamie Post had bragged about the care packages and it made Mike a little envious.

"Got a little something sweet on the side there?"

"Ol' man's got a little missus back home waiting for him!"

"Is it your birthday? Who gets to do the honors for the spankings?"

"Got yourself a lady friend, Griff?"

"What are you morons prattling on about?" Griffin asked and then looked at the box sitting there on his bunk in the corner.

"Well, I'll be..." Radar sat beside Griffin, her tail wagging happily before barking. "What? You think this is for you?

C'mon up here," he ordered, patting on the bunk as the dog took her seat beside the officer.

"It's from the kid. You guys want to see if she sent more Twinkies?" Griffin suddenly smiled making him look a bit more approachable. Everyone quickly surrounded Griffin and leaned over to see what was in the box as he opened it before a chorus of groans rose up around Mike.

There were puppy treats, drawing pencils, paper, envelopes and stamps. The bottom of the large box revealed another box of Twinkies – but there was also Chapsticks, a large bag of beef jerky, a few lottery scratch-off tickets and toiletries. Pine scented body wash, deodorant, and shampoo. Small packages of chewing gum had been hastily shuffled everywhere in the mix of goodies.

The box was large and barely anyone got packages, much less letters anymore. Mail was precious and packages were infinitely more so. Generously, Griffin began handing out packages of gum to everyone until he ran out. Mike accepted the pack of gum and a scratch ticket gratefully.

"If you win? I'm mailing it back to her," Griffin ordered with a pointed look, before sitting down to read the letter in the envelope that had been stuffed inside. Mike popped a piece of cinnamon gum into his mouth and sat down there on the metal footlocker beside Post.

"Read it out loud!" was shouted and Griffin nodded.

Mike watched stunned and in utter fascination as a bevy of expressions crossed the older man's face before he smelled the paper. Was it perfumed? Gosh there was nothing better than the scent of perfume on a woman, Mike sighed and realized it had been a few years since he'd been out with a girl.

"That's not from a kid, is it?" Post asked suddenly beside Mike, staring at Griffin.

"No."

"Read it out loud, Griff."

Griffin cleared his throat and began to speak. Mike listened utterly fascinated and a little jealous that having a pen-pal brought such happiness to the whole group. He wasn't sure that he could share his letters, feeling suddenly selfish and realizing again what a giving man that his commanding officer could be.

MR. GRIFFIN AND RADAR,

I truly enjoyed your letter and drawing. It almost looked like your shepherd signed the paper herself, I was so impressed. I am glad you and your friends enjoyed the Twinkies – they are a favorite of mine. I am a teacher at the elementary school that sent the letters out, so I will accept your thanks as well as pass on your story to my parents and my students. Perhaps you can use the drawing pencils and pad to hone your skills drawing. You truly have a gift for it. I hope you can use a few of the items, if not, please distribute them out and know that we all pray for your continued safety back in the States. Is there anything you particularly need or would like? You mentioned greenery from home, so I've included a few things that made me think of trees. I've enjoyed your letter and it brought a smile to a dull day.

Thank you again- and be safe.

Lily

P.S. I've included some postage for you as well as paper/envelopes in hopes that we might continue our correspondence. God bless.

SEVERAL OF THE men began patting Griffin on the shoulder and laughing, teasing him about the drawing skills that he apparently had hidden deep down inside. Post gave Griffin a high five and muttered about how Annabelle, his fiancée, never wrote him anymore. Feeling exceptionally happy and a part of the group, Mike saw Griffin was practically blushing at the attention he was receiving. Standing up, Mike grabbed his CPO and kissed him on the cheek playfully, mocking him as he sang "Oooooh Griffin, you ol' stud, you!" in a sing song voice.

Mike never saw Griffin's fist coming until it connected with his nose.

Stunned, Mike felt the sharp explosion of pain and nearly blacked out before muttering several curse words that was garbled by the blood he suddenly tasted in his mouth. Mike felt a strong hand grab him by the scruff of his shirt as he was practically dragged out of the tent into the blinding sun, making the pain ten times worse. He blindly walked along, afraid to touch his nose. A sudden veiling of darkness revealed that they'd entered another tent causing Mike to crack open an eye as he saw the corpsman, Houghton, standing in front of them with a frown on his face.

"What happened?" Houghton questioned.

"I had a problem and took care of it," Griffin said evasively standing nearby.

"Cooper - is that correct?"

"Yes sir, I jumped in front of his fist," Mike smarted off with a bloodied smile, looking at his CPO, who was now grinning at him.

"And you? Your hand magically discovered his broken nose?"

"Oh no sir, it was worse. I fell into his face when I tripped."

"I see," the nurse rolled his eyes and handed them icepacks. Mike gingerly touched the cold surface to his nose and flinched, causing it to scrunch up again involuntarily, causing more pain. "You two are incorrigible and will be hurting something fierce."

Houghton walked off in disgust. Griffin turned to Mike, chuckling lightly the moment they were alone. Mike was certain that the older officer absolutely hated him but now he wasn't so sure. It was like they were finally developing some sort of camaraderie and for Mike – he sincerely hoped so. Deep down inside, he wanted to be a part of something greater than he was and to fit in – both of which he felt was strained right now. He was the new guy, the kid of the group, and the pest.

"Let's get one thing straight: You ever kiss me again and I will break both my hands next time. Are we clear?"

"Sir? May I speak freely?"

"Go ahead."

"Chicks like men with character but no more playing around, I swear it. The ladies like rugged and I figured you scored me a girl next time I'm on leave, eh?" Unfortunately for Mike, due to the broken nose it sounded almost unintelligible as he spoke. *'Mix wike men wif character. Ice wear id. Core me a curl ex time I'm on weave'.*

"Sure kid." Griffin smiled. "Now, you might have two black eyes if you don't keep that icepack on there and stay quiet."

"Got it," Mike mumbled erratically and put the icepack against his face again. "Are we good?" he asked and then frowned as he heard himself. It sounded like he'd said *'arf we wood?'*

"Yeah, Cooper – we're good," Griffin admitted quietly. Mike opened his eyes momentarily to see the respect in the other man's eyes. He put the icepack back on his nose and gave a blind thumbs up to his CPO before groaning at the pain in his face.

CHAPTER 2

2 015

"BECCA? BECCA? ARE YOU HERE?" Cora said aloud to the nearly empty apartment that she shared with her roommate. She'd taken on the tenant in order to help make ends meet as a suggestion she'd seen online. It worked for other people, why not her? Problem was that Becca was consistently late with the rent the last three months and Cora suspected her of doing drugs. She didn't plan on renewing the contract nor allowing her the chance to stay the other nine months. She'd drawn up eviction papers just to be on the safe side in case things got ugly.

They were ugly now.

Cora didn't have a lot in her life and what she did have, she scraped together the funds to make sure it was paid for. She didn't need extra expenses or a ton of bills. That just ate at her and made her feel anxious knowing it would be coming due. She liked to pay for things outright and was so proud of her apartment. It was small, clean, and furnished with things that made her feel good about herself. Her home was her haven – and now it was gone.

Horrified, she stared at the scattered remaining contents of her apartment and the damage that had been done to the walls, flooring, and even the ceiling. The large gouges in the wood laminate was the first thing that drew the eye but then the gaping holes and missing light fixtures completed the masterpiece of destruction before her. Everything was gone. Her couch, her end tables, her television, her computer - everything.

Her knees gave out as her mind raced. Cora fell hard onto the flooring and winced as a splinter drove right into the skin of her knee. Rising to her feet, she absently looked in Becca's door that was ajar, praying for some sort of explanation. Her room was empty and the walls were spray painted with graffiti. *How could this happen,* Cora wondered in shock. She'd been stressed all day about forgetting her purse at home only to come home from work to suddenly discover *this*!

Looking into her own bedroom, she collapsed again in a cry of sheer disbelief. Her full-size bed had been dismantled, the windowpane looking out on the alleyway was broken, and everything else was gone – including her chest of drawers that contained a pouch with a few pieces of costume jewelry she'd collected over the years at garage sales. If everything was gone, then so was her checkbook and her only credit card.

"No," she whispered in the silence and reached for her cellphone in her pocket. Pulling it out, she called 911. "My name is Cora Dillion and I've been robbed."

Cora was still sitting in the same place on her bedroom floor when the police arrived. They took photos, recording everything, and took Cora's statement. They asked for photos of Becca but she didn't have any. The copy of the rental contract was gone, as well as any possible information she had to give them.

"Miss, I would recommend you contact your bank, the complex, and your insurance immediately. Get a hotel room for the night and see if you can get yourself settled into another place with different locks. They are going to want to get this apartment repaired immediately so they can rent it out again. You won't want to stay here with it like this," the officer told her kindly.

Cora nodded, stupefied, and felt panic welling up inside of her. She called her bank and listened numbly as they told her that she'd just closed her account. Cora shut her eyes against the surging pressure that was throbbing behind her eyes. She was going to have a migraine. Becca had her license, her social security card and her cash now.

The property manager came walking in, claiming to have seen the police lights in the parking lot. She took one look around and focused right on Cora.

"Have you called your insurance company?"

"I don't have rental insurance," Cora whispered blankly. She'd cut it off six months ago because she was having a hard time making ends meet. Desperation had made her jump at the opportunity to save fifty bucks a month, which still wasn't enough to get by. Financial woes were the reason she'd taken in a tenant.

"What happened?"

"My roommate took..."

"Your *roommate*? You aren't supposed to have anyone else living here. There is no one else on your contract," Mrs. Stivers, the property manager, said harshly. The next few hours were a conglomeration of nightmarish events spiraling out of control.

Cora was suddenly homeless for breach of contract, unable to put down a deposit on another place to rent, nor could she prove who she was. Sleeping in her car that night, she went to a nearby coffee shop to wash her face and straightened her clothing before going into work to talk with her boss.

She cashed out her 401k and took the penalty, reducing the amount she thought she was going to get into half. She had to call them to arrange to send a check to another location, desperately afraid that if she sent it to the apartment that Becca would steal that too.

Angry, humiliated, and feeling desperate – Cora knew that she would never forget the lesson that she'd been taught, nor could she stay there in Dallas where everyone was practically strangers. She wanted a small-town life where everyone knew each other. She wanted to feel safe and not have to look over her shoulder all the time, where she could afford to live on her own, and not have to worry about running into Becca. She'd never felt such bitter hatred towards someone and wasn't sure how to cope with the feelings inside her right now.

She had to get away and knew that she would never let anyone into her world again. She couldn't rely, or trust anyone ever again – no one but herself.

GHAZNI, Afghanistan

MIKE'S EARS rang horribly after hearing the explosion nearby. Stunned, he looked around and saw the shock and disbelief on the rest of his teams faces. Some of them had been knocked back by the blast. Minter the Moron, the biggest dork out there (*next to him, of course*) that he adored like a brother, was lying on the ground screaming.

He saw the wild panicked look on Wilkes' face and the instant wave of guilt on Griffin's – knowing the older man instantly blamed himself for letting one of them get hurt. He put on a tough guy act but was really a softy on the inside and Mike knew that now.

"Ethan! I'm here! Minter, I've got you!" Wilkes screamed, scrambling over to where Minter was lying on the ground. Several men were scrambling in the dirt, trying to get to Minter, but Cooper couldn't move

"Look at me! Look here! Look at me, brother!"

It was nauseating to look at the carnage in front of him. There was blood everywhere. Ethan's leg lay off in the distance, barely recognizable. Mike never considered himself a wuss, but the scene in front of him wasn't from the movies or any sort of special effects – this was real.

He couldn't help the wrenching nausea that suddenly hit him as Minter's life was ebbing away in the sand before his very eyes. Mike threw up several times in the sand, unable to stop himself. His eyes burned with tears and even Post collapsed in the dirt onto his knees in shock. They all knew Ethan Minter was going to bleed out there in the Afghan desert.

"Keep him looking at you," Griffin screamed at Wilkes. The older man stood up and yanked off his belt, trying to knot a tourniquet on Ethan's leg to stop the bleeding. Radar, the K9 bomb dog, was whining and circling the men warily. "Don't let him look at me, Wilkes! You got that? Minter you aren't going to die like this!"

"Keep talking to him, Wilkes." CPO Griffin ordered harshly as he picked up Minter bodily. Ethan's head lolled back and Wilkes was clutching at Minter's hand desperately. "Let's go! Now! Move it!"

Everyone was racing back towards the direction they'd come from as fast as they could move in the blistering heat. They were in full gear and the only thing pushing them was adrenaline and fear. Mike thought about shucking his heavy pack on his back if he had to throw up again but he didn't want to leave anything there in the desert for someone else to find.

"Keep talking Wilkes! Don't let him go!"

"Ethan you hear that?" Wilkes yelled at Minter's listless form. "We've got you, man. You're gonna be okay!"

Time moved in slow motion and Mike felt like it was taking forever to get back to base. Post grabbed Mike's elbow as they ran at one point to keep him on his feet. Mike couldn't look anywhere but the sand in front of him. He couldn't look at Minter or the hysteria on Wilkes' face. Fifteen minutes later, Minter was in a room, away from prying eyes, and had finally stopped the horrific screaming. The silence was deafening and covered the area around the small building with dread.

"Is he... dead?" Wilkes whispered fearfully.

"No, they gave him morphine and knocked him out so they could close off the wound," Mike muttered, feeling a wave of nausea rise up again in his stomach from where he sat on the ground outside of the building. They were all sitting on the ground, waiting, as if their legs couldn't hold them any longer.

"Man, that was brutal," Mike kept repeating, shaking his head in disbelief. He was desperately trying not to vomit again for two reasons. He was afraid he'd end up with dehydration – which could be fatal here – and he was trying to keep his dignity intact so that way he didn't revert to being *'the pest'* or *'kid'* again. He was finally feeling like he belonged with this group and he loved them all like family.

"He's alive," Post said firmly, putting a hand on Colin's

shoulder where he sat beside him in the dirt. "Minter's gonna make it. He's too stubborn to die. Are you okay, Wilkes?"

"No," Colin admitted painfully, "I don't think I will ever be the same again."

Mike understood that and met Post's eyes. No one would ever forget today and they all felt emotionally scarred in different ways.

"WILKES! GET BACK HERE MAN!" Mike yelled out in disbelief as he spotted Wilkes up a rocky hill while the others were down here in formation.

"Are you trying to *find* a bomb out there?" Cooper snapped at him, feeling an uncontrollable rage overwhelm him as he tapped on Wilkes' helmet angrily. The sheer disregard for his own safety blew Mike's mind.

He couldn't have something like that happen again while he was present. To Mike, his world was falling apart before his very eyes and spinning out of control. Griffin had actually declined reenlistment and moved to Texas. Mike had written Ethan an email but never really heard much back. Mike knew he was alive, but not much else.

"You know, if you step on one you might not make it out alive like Minter did. It's not a contest, man. You don't have to blow off your leg like him," Mike hollered painfully and realized that he'd gone too far. The men around him got silent and you could have heard a pin drop.

Learning from experience, Mike leaned back and nearly fell over from the weight of his pack, as he saw Wilkes draw back to punch him. Flinching he expected to feel his nose break again any second now and realized wryly that he was going to have to learn control of his mouth someday.

"You take that back!" Colin Wilkes roared.

"It's the truth!" Mike hollered, just as upset as the man before him obviously was. His whole demeanor had changed and his face was flushed bright red in anger.

"I'm just angry enough to say it to your face. All of us see it and nobody wants to haul your butt out of here," Mike admitted candidly. "Dude, you are the biggest guy in the pack. What are you, three hundred pounds of muscle?"

"I'm not trying to get even with Minter, you idiot!"

"And I'm not trying to get a massive hernia dragging your bleeding carcass out of some sand filled canyon. My *junk* is precious to me," Mike said bluntly to the bigger man, pointing at his own pants. A few guys snickered around where they stood. He was serious and beyond caring right now. He would not, could not, watch another man die from sheer stupidity and carelessness.

"Now if the other guys want to carry you out- fine! Keep going off on your own towards the places we haven't swept for landmines yet. Boys - let's see a show of hands. Anyone want to drag Wilkes' six-foot and five-inch frame back to camp in this unbearable heat?" Mike asked plainly, feeling a wave of regret for the man as silence surrounded him. Since when had he become the voice of reason? He wanted to be the lighthearted guy that he tried to portray to the outside world. It was easier to fake being happy than to face the overwhelming despair he felt constantly.

Colin stood there dumbstruck.

"I rest my case. Man, we love you… but you got a death wish and you're too careless for your own good. You gotta pay attention and let whatever is going on in your head – you *gotta* let it go."

"Cooper's right," Post admitted. "Let's move out, men."

2016

"CORA, ARE YOU PLAYING CANDY CRUSH?" Ava asked her quietly in the breakroom of the insurance office they worked at. Taking a bite of her peanut butter sandwich, Cora nodded quickly and went back to playing. It was none of the woman's business what she was doing during her lunch break.

Truthfully, Cora was so lucky to have this job right now and would play nice with her coworkers as much as required. She wasn't letting anyone in her world again – ever! Being homeless for two weeks and sleeping in her car was the most horrific thing she'd ever gone through. It was such a quick brutal slip down a slope she'd never anticipated and she was still in the process of recovering a year later.

"Shoot," Cora muttered as her time ran out and she was out of lives. Now Ava would want to talk to her if she wasn't busy. Ava was nice enough and Cora knew a little about her, but that was about it. She drove a red Honda, had a baby girl named Aurora, went to the same therapist as Cora, and was talking to some guy online. The therapist was almost a necessary evil in her life because Cora had never been able to get past the utter devastation and betrayal.

She was scared and someone jerked her security blanket out from under her. Growing up, she was an only child and her dad ran off before she was born. Her mother had passed away when she was fifteen and she'd been on her own since. She had distant relatives but wasn't close with them. Her mother had runaway as a girl and never looked back – thus estranging Cora as well from her distant family.

"Do you play Candy Crush a lot?"

"Why?"

"I've got this guy I'm talking to and his friend is always playing," Ava began but Cora shut her down immediately.

"I don't want to date anyone."

"I'm not asking you to."

"Then what are you getting at?"

"I thought that maybe you two could exchange emails or letters – or whatever you do in Candy Crush and send each other lives or treats. I don't play the game so I'm not a hundred percent sure – but I know that Cooper is all over it and talks to Colin about it all the time."

"Do you know what level he's on?"

"I've got no clue."

"And you aren't setting me up?"

"Gosh no – the man is in the military and all the way in Afghanistan."

"He's across the globe, not looking for anything from me, and plays Candy Crush?" Cora mused silently as she stared at Ava trying to get a read on her. If the woman was lying, she'd be extremely upset and probably start looking for another job since she couldn't handle betrayal anymore in any fashion. She was still putting herself back together and it had been a long, arduous battle she'd fought mentally and financially. In fact, Cora was still sleeping on a twin bed on the floor of her studio apartment, since she was unable to buy a bedframe or more furniture just yet.

"He's really nice and I promise – he's just into Candy Crush. That's all."

Sighing heavily, Cora looked at her cell phone and saw she had another thirteen minutes until she earned back a single life on the game. Her phone was several years old and had to last as long as possible. This silly, addictive game was her only consolation and enjoyment in the rare bit of free time that she allowed herself.

"Give me his name and email," Cora conceded and

instantly felt wary as Ava's face blossomed into a huge smile. "I might look him up or contact him – *might, maybe, possibly* – but I'm not making any promises!"

"No problem. I will drop him a line and tell him to be on his best behavior or else," Ava promised, smiling happily at Cora.

"This is a friend of the guy that was working on your car in the parking lot last month?"

"Yes."

"And he's a good guy – that guy you are talking to?"

"Colin is the best," Ava said dreamily, closing her eyes. Cora stared at her and felt a surge of jealousy flare inside of her. "Colin is sweet, caring, protective but not pushy in the slightest. It's like he is just happy being with me or taking care of me. I miss him terribly and hope he is safe in Afghanistan."

"He's there with your Candy Crush buddy?"

"Mike Cooper – and yes. Mike is in the same barracks and does explosives just like Colin. All of those guys in that group are super sweet. I should introduce you sometime to a few of them next time I get a chance. Ethan, John, Colin, Mike, Jamie... well, you get my drift – there are a lot of them. Mike is the 'Candy Crush buddy', as you have dubbed him."

"And this Mike guy isn't a creep – none of them are?" Cora asked warily. "I will admit that it was really touching to see your guy taking care of your brakes for you and it surprised me."

"I promise you – they are all really good people."

"You better not be lying to me," Cora whispered painfully, staring at Ava as she smiled encouragingly at her. Ava laid her hand on Cora's arm and nodded.

"I understand," Ava said softly. "They are good and you..."

"Don't say *'trust me'* because that phrase is the kiss of death right there," Cora interrupted. "I will think about emailing this Mike Cooper guy but if I do – it's not because I believe you or trust you. It's because I want to or need another life for my game."

Ava blinked in surprise and looked shocked at Cora's harsh words, making Cora immediately soften her tone since she had to continue working here for now. She liked this job and it paid halfway decently. The hours were good and it gave her more time to focus on building her own business so she could become self-sufficient and never worry again about money.

"It's not personal – I have some serious trust issues."

"You and me both, but for different reasons."

"Do you want to share your personal demons?"

"Not any more than you do," Cora retorted and nodded politely. "Just put his info on a sticky note when you get a few minutes."

"That's all I could ask."

Cora sat in front of her old computer and waited for it to boot up. The unit was on its last legs but it needed to work for a while longer. Cora was willing to nurse it along as long as she had to. The desktop computer was purchased at a Goodwill store and she had to replace some of the memory cards, but it still functioned. The monitor was an old thick boxy tube monitor with a radiant green circle in the upper left corner of the screen indicating where it was going bad too. The monitor was free and the computer cost her all of eighty dollars – so she was willing to deal with its quirks to try and get ahead.

Cora was brilliant with creating websites and troubleshooting problems online. She did contract work from her home for extra money. The computer and monitor were set up on a flimsy desk in the corner of the living room that was adjacent to her bedroom loft area.

None of her stuff was in excellent condition but it was hers and it was paid for. She was making progress from the girl that had to sell plasma to buy groceries and clothing that first month that she was getting started again. That girl was long gone. She vowed she would never have to do something like that again.

As the computer finally came on and connected to the internet, Cora sighed. She had no idea what to say to this guy. She'd been staring at the sticky note repeatedly, wondering if she should send out an email or not. Truthfully, she was stuck on the same level of Candy Crush and couldn't get past it right now. She needed some gifts on the game and could use a few extra lives. Truthfully, what she needed was a shoulder to cry on at times, and she was terrified to let anyone in.

MR. COOPER,

I received your email address and name from Ava Buchannan – I believe she is acquainted with a friend of yours, Colin Wilkes. She requested I reach out to you because we both enjoy a common game and truthfully – I could use some help.

I'm stuck on level seven hundred and forty-one and can't get past that cursed maze. I've got some pink goo that keeps swallowing up the blocks and reminds me a lot of how I am feeling right now.

Every time I turn around – I've got some other nightmare just waiting to drag me down. Life just sucks. I wish there was some magical speckled candy that could make everything better or wipe the slate clean just so I could sleep at night or function. I feel completely pathetic that I am reaching out to a stranger on the other side of the world but I have no one here I can rely on. I've learned my lesson there – the hard way!

I just need a bit of help, you know?

I'm tired of being kicked while I'm down and things have been rough lately. I can't concentrate and keep having to wait for another life every chance I play the game... so how about you and I exchange lives, tokens, candies, and emails – and maybe I can finally beat the level.

Sincerely,

Cora Dillion

Ps – What level <u>are</u> you on anyhow?

4

GHAZNI, Afghanistan

MIKE WAITED IMPATIENTLY for his turn at the shared computer. He hadn't received an email from his new pen-pal last week and he hoped that he would get one this week. It was a real drag having to wait for your assigned time to use the computer or waiting for it to free up. He played the game as much as he could and sometimes snuck in to simply earn more candies in the game by logging in daily. If he couldn't play, he was at least going to throw everything he could into the game when he did get his turn finally.

Truthfully, it wasn't so much the game that he enjoyed – it was the blissful numbness that focusing on the screen brought to his thoughts. He was still having nightmares of Minter losing his leg.

That could have been any one of them.

He couldn't blame Wilkes because they all played around at various times simply to let off steam. Now Wilkes had been suspended and Post just got news that his fiancée had been fooling around on him making him not fit to talk to. He didn't want to hear about *Annabelle-this* or *Annabelle-that*. Post wasn't dumb and the girl had him completely fooled while she fleeced him for every cent he was earning. He felt sorry for the man – heck, he felt sorry for all of them! He was surrounded by a bunch of guys completely down in the dumps.

As the chair finally emptied, Mike slid into it with exaggerated relief and sighed dramatically for good measure. It was an unspoken rule here that you didn't go over your hour nor did you take another guy's timeslot. You could end up with a 'blanket party' if you weren't careful – and he had no desire to get smothered with a blanket and beat with a brick of soap dangling from some sweaty tube sock. Nooooo thank you!

Loading up his email, he did a cursory sweep looking for any word from the outside world. Griffin still sent an occasional email and he'd finally heard from Minter. The guy sounded like he was really getting his life back in order and Mike was glad to hear it. Scrolling farther down through the junk emails, he stopped and did a double take.

CDILLION?

CLICKING ON THE EMAIL, he began to read the screen and stopped. He took a deep breath, re-read the computer monitor, and tried to relax as he felt a clenching in his chest. How could someone understand or know what was on his mind? He was feeling exactly the same way.

No matter what he did, something seemed to keep happening around him. It was only a matter of time before he got swallowed up by the nightmare around him. Mentally, he likened it to a man being thrown overboard in an ocean with utterly nothing in sight – but he really liked her analogy of the pink goo swallowing up everything too. He hated that level of the game with a passion!

Cora,

I am so glad you've written. I'm on level nine-hundred and forty-two but that is only because I get computer time once a week or sneak in the computer room when I can. I'd be more than happy to send you some lives, candies, or power-ups. I try to go out of my way to pass the building just to dart inside, log in, get my free stuff and then give up the computer to the next yahoo that is up for his assigned timeslot. It's a pretty good gig and has me fully stocked with treasures to share with my new Candy Crush buddy! I will log in on the game momentarily and set you up royally – get ready!

Ava is more than just a friend with my boy, Wilkes. I think they have something special going. He's a pretty good guy when he isn't completely ga-ga over Ava or her baby. The man makes the sappiest faces when he is looking over her photos... truthfully, it makes me a little jealous.

Getting your email has truly been the best thing that has happened to me in months. I know... that sounds pathetic and lonely. It's the truth though. I miss having someone to talk to and cut up with – it's just not the same as talking with the guys. I am so relieved that you wrote me.

It's the 'bomb-diggity'! (Cora - check your game – I sent you several bombs to clear the board. That should get you past that pink goop level. I really hate that screen.) What about you? Write back – tell me all about you. I will try to sneak in, send a few more quick emails, and let me know what you need for your game.

~Mike

. . .

NERVOUSLY, Mike re-read his email before clicking send. It was hard to explain just how happy he felt in getting a silly email. He'd meant every word when he said that he felt keenly happy at seeing her name. He knew that he was really being dragged down emotionally and mentally by the atmosphere here. Everything was a reminder of Minter being discharged. In fact, he was nearly surrounded with new faces. Griffin, Minter, now Wilkes... even Post was in a foul mood.

He wanted something to look forward to, something that felt welcoming or inviting. The thought of having a friend, a buddy, that was just his – someone he didn't have to worry about disappointing or commit a lot of time to seemed to be just the thing he needed.

The fact that it was a woman, didn't go unnoticed or unappreciated.

Mike was actually very envious of how some of his friends were finding that special someone. He craved the idea of having someone that simply 'got' him. It wasn't *'Mike the dumb kid'*, or *'Cooper the rookie'*... but rather he got this insane craving of wanting to hear someone say his name with that special tone in their voice. He wanted to hold someone's hand, go to a movie with someone to share a moment or simply hang out. In a sea of sand, surrounded by soldiers, Mike realized the truth.

He was lonely.

CORA SAT at her makeshift desk staring at the screen frowning. There was a glitch somewhere in the code that glared brightly on the display making the webpage she was designing look completely wonky. She'd been going through it line by line for almost an hour now, irritated beyond measure. Glancing up at the clock, she realized it was nearing midnight and she needed to go to bed soon.

Leaning back, she rubbed her eyes and arched her head back. Someday she hoped her work came to fruition. She wanted to be able to never worry about money again. The idea of having a nest egg that was just her own, something she could rely on for security was something she craved beyond measure. That moment from a few years ago still burned brightly in her mind, making her sick to her stomach. That insidious fear had taken root and grown, causing her to be afraid of anyone offering help. What if they had ulterior motives and were simply trying to take advantage of a gullible woman once again?

Sighing heavily, she saved the screen and began to close the windows she had open on her computer, one by one. As she clicked on the X in the right hand corner of the window for her Gmail screen, her eyes glanced down and caught the fact that she'd received an email. It registered in her mind seconds after she'd closed the screen, making her immediately reopen another one.

Sure enough, she had an email from Mike Cooper.

Scrolling through the email, she felt her heart hammering in her chest as she realized that this stranger across the world might actually be nice to keep in touch with. He seemed to be very relaxed, outgoing, and friendly … but safely thousands of miles away from her.

Opening up her Candy Crush game, Cora gaped in shock. He'd sent her ten bombs that would clear most of her screen when she used them. Those little candy bombs were expensive and you had to wait patiently to get them one per day. How could he simply give them away? – and to her, a stranger?

Hitting reply, Cora drafted up a simple email in case Mike was still online. She was stunned by his generosity and wanted to say thank you immediately, especially since he only got the computer once a week. Having him for a Candy Crush friend would obviously make her game a lot easier to level up, especially if he was this giving. He'd be awfully disappointed if he expected the same from her, she thought, feeling that bit of wariness creep into her mind.

HELLO MIKE – thank you so much for the candy bombs for the game. Wow! I can't believe you had that many to give away so easily. I'm incredibly cheap and don't purchase the extras in the game, which is part of the reason I could use some help. I'm glad you emailed. I will send you another email when I can, but it's nearing midnight here and I've got work tomorrow.

Thanks again!

Cora

... AND THE REASON I am not sending any your way either, Cora thought in embarrassment at the constant lack of funds she faced in between paychecks. She got by but there wasn't enough cushion to be comfortable. Maintaining her website for her side business was expensive and she was desperately hording away as many funds as possible to invest in a new computer.

Feeling a bit more chipper, she clicked send on the email. It was time she went to bed before that insidious small voice in her head could plague her with doubt and cause her not to respond at all. Why would someone be so generous or nice for no reason at all? People weren't nice for simply no reason, or so she'd found. Everyone had an agenda it seemed; it was just a matter of finding out what his was.

EARLY THE NEXT MORNING, Cora went through her day routinely. As she sat in the breakroom alone, she loaded up her game and played on her phone. Dropping several of the little candy bombs onto the board, she whipped through the level in five moves. Little bursts appeared all over the board, causing the rows to drop or collapse as each line cleared methodically. Grinning, she watched the score soar in the upper corner and nearly jumped out of her seat when the next screen loaded.

"Oh, thank goodness!" she sighed dramatically and blindly picked up her bologna sandwich to take a bite.

"Yes, yes – I usually tend to have that effect when I walk into a room," Ava teased sarcastically. Cora actually felt herself genuinely happy to see the woman that worked on the opposite side of the office. "What are you so happy about?"

"I beat the level I was stuck on."

"Oh, you did? That's great I guess," Ava shrugged and took a seat nearby. "I don't play so I'm happy for you, but I really have no clue as to how hard the game is. So, yay! Go Cora!"

"Thank you. I'm more relieved cause it's a different screen now instead of that same one over and over again."

"Yeah, monotony is a pretty horrible thing."

"Very much so," Cora agreed immediately. "How is your daughter doing with daycare?"

"She's good," Ava responded and then smiled guiltily. "She's good, I'm not. I'd rather spend my days at home with her since we're actually fitting into a routine now. She's getting to be fun instead of a little poop-machine."

"I've heard of cherubs, little dolls, and cutie pies – but poop-machine is a new one for me," Cora admitted lightly.

"That's because you haven't changed one of her diapers."

"Let's keep it that way too."

"The only person she adores more than me, seems to be Colin."

"That's good, isn't it?"

"Very. He's just – wait! Did Mike ever email you?"

"Yesterday," Cora confessed, feeling her cheeks heat up with embarrassment. "He seems pretty nice and gave me several candy bombs for the game that got me past the level."

"Is he nice? He seems to be and Colin thinks highly of him."

"I thought you knew the guy?"

"I know he wants a pen-pal and is lonely – but that is really it. I don't *know* him myself. Just a friend of a friend, that's all. If he gives you bad vibes, just blow him off. You aren't going to hurt my feelings."

"So, what's his deal? Why does he want to write to someone?"

"Bored and wants a gamer friend?"

"No, seriously – what's his real agenda?"

"What do you mean?"

"Someone is always out to get something. You made it seem like you knew him, well, several of the guys, and that he was okay – but now I find out that you barely know the guy. Obviously, you wanted me to write him. Why? What's in it for you?"

Ava stared at Cora in surprise.

"Not everyone has an agenda. If you think he has one, ask him. Obviously you don't mince words when you think someone's trying to pull a fast one – which I am not. If Colin tells me that he is a good guy, I am going to assume so because I think Colin is a really nice person, but my seal of approval means nothing to anyone but me. If you want to write him, great. I'm happy for you. If not, then don't and I will still talk with my coworker when we have lunch together. Now," Ava said, getting up from her seat and staring down at Cora, "I think I'm suddenly not very hungry and you need to think about what you expect from people."

Cora watched the door close behind Ava, leaving her alone in the breakroom once again. She'd been meeting with a counselor occasionally when she could afford to go, simply because she knew she had trust issues. Daisy suggested she step slowly out of her comfort zone and make a few friends, but with boundaries in order to keep from feeling scared or running away. She hadn't really focused on the advice too much because Cora hadn't realized just how jaded she actually was until Ava practically tossed it in her face.

Daisy, her counselor, was right.

Cora needed to try to work on making friends and get past the initial instinct to protect herself. She'd offended Ava and that was the sole person she actually communicated with at work in the office. She avoided speaking with anyone else, brushing it off as true dedication to her job. But that wasn't it at all; Cora was terrified someone would discover something to use against her to make others dislike her or get her fired.

Ava had been kind enough to suggest someone to befriend with no strings attached. She'd never pushed or pried into her private life – nor had she asked anything of her. She owed Ava an apology and owed it to herself to put forth an effort to make friends just so she wasn't quite so utterly alone in her world. She would take the time to write Mike an email each evening simply to say hello and thank him again.

Getting to her feet, Cora cleaned up her things and dropped her phone into her purse. Taking a deep breath, she walked into the office and listened to the faint clicking of people typing nearby. They worked in an insurance office and processed claims. The sounds were soothing, making her think of her own time she spent at the keyboard away from work. The clicking also reminded her of the webpage she needed to work on again this evening. She had her night laid out for her and felt pretty pleased about it. She'd spend her evening deciphering code and emailing Mike. Walking up to Ava's cubicle, she hesitated.

"Ava," Cora interrupted, clearing her throat. She watched the woman turn and look at her, quickly closing her eyes and taking a deep breath against the fear that beat at her gently like a moth's wings.

Don't give her any information.

She'll use it against you.

You're gullible and naïve.

"You are right and I'm sorry I snapped at you. I really do appreciate you giving me Mike's email and I know you didn't have to. I know you said you weren't hungry and I don't blame you – but I'd like to have my lunch buddy back. How about I get us some coffee?"

"I'd love a cup," Ava said quietly, smiling. "I brought in some fancy creamer this morning that I thought I'd share. Do you like cinnamon?"

"I'm more of a 'whatever-is-on-sale' kinda girl," Cora said evasively.

"With the cost of formula – me too! This is my single guilty splurge," Ava grinned. "C'mon. I think they just brewed a fresh pot and if we are lucky, there won't be any grounds in the bottom."

"Mmmm fiber," Cora mocked ruefully as Ava got to her feet. She felt a burst of relief in her as Ava linked arms with Cora.

"I was never mad at you. A bit hurt, yes," Ava whispered, "I don't have many friends and I consider you one. I can't tell you what to do or force you to do something against your will. Having a friend or pen-pal has to be completely up to you and your decision. I don't handle confrontation very well and I'm working on that, so you'll have to forgive me for getting upset and leaving the room."

"Don't apologize," Cora stammered in surprise at the candidness in the woman's voice. Cora knew Ava's history and was taken aback to hear her voice it so truthfully.

"Then don't be afraid to speak up for yourself ever," Ava said sagely. "I wish I was as bold as you sometimes. I think we could teach each other a lot as friends."

"I'd like that," Cora said genuinely.

THAT WEEKEND, Cora surprised herself several times over. She found a way to crack the coding that was causing the error on the webpage. Once it was finished, she happily billed the person and breathed a sigh of relief as she received in payment for two hundred dollars. She hadn't expected the person to pay quite so quickly nor have them tip her on top of the fee.

Instead of playing her game all weekend, Cora took some of the money to the store to get a new external hard drive to back up some of her information on the computer so if it failed, she wouldn't lose everything.

While at the store, she saw a display for Candy Crush gummy snacks and picked up a box immediately – for Mike. She wasn't big on sweets but the idea of sending him something resembling the game in lieu of reimbursing him for all the candy bombs he'd sent made her feel good. She would get an address from Ava and send it by surprise. If Colin lived near or with Mike in the barracks, it meant she could simply send it there to Colin - but address it to Mike instead.

Her mind kept drawing conclusions as to what being 'too nice' could cause, but then again – what could he do to her on the opposite side of the globe? Nothing. She knew the man's name, he knew hers, and that was it.

'Trust someone but create the boundaries you need,' Daisy had coached and she was trying hard to do that. She felt so much better after talking to Ava even if it was scary to let someone in again. Ava didn't want anything from her; she had Colin and her baby Aurora. Her car was nicer, her apartment was in a better part of town, no – Ava was safe.

Mike was an unknown and maybe she just needed to proceed with that understanding. She didn't know him, didn't trust him, and had been hurt by someone she'd considered a friend/roommate. Sitting down at her table, she poured out her thoughts and fears cathartically in an email. He'd asked about her, instructing her to tell him all about her – and she was going to do just that. She deliberately left off the email address because she wasn't sure if she would actually click send.

Dear Mike,

I am not sure why I'm doing this other that it might be something that gets me over a giant mental hurdle. I don't know why you'd want information about me because I'm just me. Nothing special. I work hard – really hard, actually and its driven by fear and lack of trust.

I don't trust anyone. I've been burnt too badly in the past and it's really damaged me. So there. You have a Candy Crush friend and pen-pal that has issues... feel free to back out now. I work full-time at the claims center with Ava but that's to pay the bills and I have no intention of being there for life. That sounds harsh but gosh... I want so much more from this broken, barren life.

CORA STOPPED AND SNIFFLED, wiping her nose, as she read

that last statement. It was brutally honest and from deep-down inside. Wiping her eyes, she continued on.

I WANT the Hallmark Channel movie of the week. I want to be free to be myself, not this frightened mockery of a woman who's looking over her shoulder all the time and double-checking herself. I'm trying so hard to make something more of myself; that I have so much more to me that is simply hidden and I want to use those talents. I started my own website a few years ago - building or repairing other websites. I'm good... really good. I want to make it take off so I have a nest egg, a cushion, some way to take care of myself when things get rough.

I have no one to depend on and that isn't a 'poor me' statement-it's the truth. I've been on my own since I was fifteen. You asked about me, so I am telling you. I'm currently twenty-six with no attachments or no grand life-events to acknowledge or share with you. I'm not a homeowner, no dog, no kids, no family, barely a jalopy of a car... but I'm going to remedy all of that someday. Period. Hallmark Channel is my goal and I think it's fairly realistic.

I don't want the moon and stars – I simply want to blossom into the person I know I can be, the one that is struggling to be discovered... and I want to remember the joy of the journey with fondness, not hatred or disgust. 'Be the best person you can be and you'll have no regrets' was what my mother always told me before she died – and I've taken that to heart.

I've always pulled back, drawn into my shell, but that has only left me lonely beyond belief. Why am I telling you this? I sound pathetic to my own ears and slightly whiney. I need a friend that doesn't need much from me because I simply don't have it in me to give.

Now, I need to get back to my next client online and fix his slider bar on his page... in fact, I am not sure I'm actually going to send this email – but then again, maybe I will simply so you know who you are dealing with because I can't see you run rolling your eyes in Afghanistan when you hit the delete key.

   Cora

CORA SIGHED HEAVILY and clicked send.

CHAPTER 3

*D*ear Mike,

Today is Friday and I feel much better. I must have been in a really rough place to have sent such a mushy email. I got the slider bar fixed on the webpage and made a cool fifty bucks to go into my savings. I hope all is well with you right now. Maybe I will simply drop a few smaller emails that are a little more upbeat. 'The Daily Life of Cora', or some garbage like that...

Friday's are my intro into the weekend and I can really spend some time at the computer plugging away because I don't have to get up early the next morning. Fridays are also 'Funky Friday' because I like to play music. Do you like music? What do you listen to? I play everything – pop, rock, country, oldies, some rap... right now I'm listening to a group called 'I Don't Know How but They Found Me' – long name, awesome songs, look it up... and you are welcome.

Cora

*H*ey *M*ike,

I know you said you get access to the computer once a week – that's rough. I keep telling myself that limited access is why you haven't written back and to quit worrying. It's Monday, which means the start to another long week of mind-numbing claims, numbers, medical jargon, and time away from my computer. In other news, guess what I discovered? I have no green thumb whatsoever. I didn't think it was possible to kill bamboo – but yeah, I did. I had three bamboo stalks in a small vase on the windowsill and they are dead. Is that a bad sign?

Cora

Hi Mike,

Omgosh I am dragging and on my fourth cup of coffee already. I worked on a complete mess last night until three in the morning and had to get up for work at six. I'm exhausted. I forgot my lunch on the counter at home, didn't charge my cell phone, and realized I wore two different shoes to work. I hope no one notices that screw up. Wish me luck getting through today cause it's barely ten in the morning and I've got about six hours left. I thought about napping in my car but I'm afraid the police would find a roasted carcass instead since it's so hot right now in Texas.

I hope the caffeine kicks in soon,

Cora

MIKE STARED at the computer screen. He felt like he'd had someone reach into his mind and pluck out his innermost thoughts as he read Cora's emails. He understood what she was saying on a level so far deep down inside of him that it was almost uncanny.

Her words, *'a broken, barren life'* resonated inside and gave him goosebumps. That was exactly how he felt but couldn't find a way to describe it. Desolate? Lost? Alone? Scared? Adrift? All of those adjectives wrapped up into one simple sentence that made his heart pound with understanding and yearning to make it better. He was freakin' stuck here for an unknown amount of time, but she was free to make her choices and change things. Why would she think he wouldn't bother to write back when he felt like someone finally understood him?

Dear Cora,

I have access for an hour today and I find myself sitting here in awe, staring at the computer screen. I get what you are saying about the Hallmark life and so very impressed by your letter.

It's okay not to trust anyone – don't let anyone ever tell you differently. Self-preservation, in any form, can never be wrong. You have to protect yourself if you feel threatened and people do it all the time. Life can be scary intense, overwhelming, or cold but that shouldn't prevent you from making friends. I hope you can consider me one.

I'm sorry to hear someone hurt you, and here if you want to unload about it. My friend got hurt and I remember what it felt like when it happened but the ripples it caused in camp were endless. I think that was part of the reason I asked for help finding a pen-pal. I needed someone to talk to and so thankful it's you.

Admittedly, when I read your words about a broken, barren life – I felt like I'd been struck dumb (Wilkes would say that I am dumb, but whatever). I want so much more too. Sand, rocks, explosives, and being alone can't be everything. I want to someday meet someone, have a home, have a family, and be part of something greater that just myself.

I'm so impressed right now that you are bettering yourself (and your life!) by developing your own business. Wow! You are an amazing, impressive woman and I am taken aback for words. You don't sound whiney or pathetic in the slightest – please don't ever think that you can't share something. I need someone to talk to and I might be wrong, but maybe you do too? It helps to unload and I hope I don't come off as a loser in my emails to you.

My buddy Post is going through some sort of fiasco back home so when I was getting ready to sneak on the computer to email you on Friday, I found out that he needed it more than I did at that moment. I've never seen the man look so shell-shocked. Post said he didn't want to talk about it but I'm going to see if I can drag it out of him without getting my nose broken again by one of the guys.

I'm twenty-six too, just FYI. Single, dark brown hair, brown eyes, with a bump on my nose from where my CPO socked me one day for making fun of him. Did I mention that I like to goof around a lot to lighten the mood?

I've never planted bamboo nor really been anywhere long enough to develop roots (get it?) but I'm hoping someday that I can. Military life can be tough but so rewarding too. I'm paid, I've got plenty of benefits, and can travel the world ... just wish I wasn't here right now. I'm hoping to get a chance to pick a different locale in the future only I don't know where I'd go.

I adore music so I will definitely look up that group. I listen to everything too - including classical. Have you seen any plays or concerts? I've seen several gigs on base when the groups come into town for an event. My favorite so far was watching Toby Keith play. When I'm feeling down, I try to listen to something peppy. I'm listening to 'Uptown Girl' right now by Billy Joel and tempted to get up, dance, and snap my fingers to the music, but I also know that if I did – I'd never hear the end of it from the guys.

Don't work too hard this weekend and share when you can. I'm heading to iTunes next to get a few songs by that group. Thank you for the suggestion and the emails. There is no way I'm hitting delete or not responding when this has been the highlight of my week, Cora.

Keep 'em coming,

Mike

"You finished, Cooper? You're cutting into my time," Parker said hotly, crossing his arms over his chest.

"Yep. I'm just sitting here to keep the chair warm for you, buddy," Mike teased and hurriedly clicked send before logging out. He didn't want to lose the email nor have anyone else read it. Perhaps he'd sneak in during the night and send Cora another one. As he walked out of the building, he realized that he'd completely forgotten to send her a Candy Crush life or extras for the game. *Maybe he would do more than just send a letter later,* he mused, smiling to himself. He'd send another series of candy bombs to her game again so she could keep playing.

Mike made it a point to walk past the building several times, peeking his head inside each time to see what the wait time was for the computer. Having assigned times was cramping his style and he was anxiously awaiting a reply from Cora or the chance to log on to the game. Every time he went past, there were usually two or three men waiting for their turn.

Walking to the Exchange store that was on site, Mike stopped in to get another uniform shirt for himself. The last one had lost a button and tore at the pocket. As he stood there waiting to pay, he glanced around and saw a small charm on a chain in the case next to several keychains, knives, and compasses. The charm was a tiny compass engraved on a disc. It looked almost like a starburst until you saw the tiny initials indicating the direction that North and South were in.

"Is this all for you today, Cooper?" the clerk asked him as he set his shirt onto the counter. Mike glanced back down at the case and hesitated. It was awfully personal to send a gift right away and they were barely acquaintances, but it just seemed so fitting to see something like that out of the blue.

"I'll take the little necklace too."

"That for you?"

"Ha ha. Very funny, Wilson. Don't you have something better to do with your time other than harass a paying customer?"

"Yep. I can take your hard-earned money," the clerk named Wilson said chuckling. "That'll be ninety-eight dollars."

"What?"

"The shirt is twenty-five bucks and your little piece of jewelry plus Uncle Sam's cut makes up the balance. Want me to put it back?"

"No."

"I didn't think so, lover boy. Get your girl something pretty and she'll put up with your ugly mug for a while longer."

"Shut up Wilson and just run my card, will ya?"

"With pleasure, Coop."

Tucking the little box in his pocket, Mike walked out of the Exchange store and stopped in his tracks. His shoulders slumped as his whole demeanor sagged in defeat. He'd picked up the little necklace without thinking the whole thing through. He didn't even have Cora's address and she openly told him that she didn't trust anyone.

Asking for something as personal as where she lived was sure to be a hard 'no' from her. He'd wait to mail it to Cora until Wilkes got back from his suspension – and then send it to Ava's address to give to Cora. The last thing he wanted was to come off as intrusive or prying... or even desperate. He really liked what he'd read so far and it only piqued his curiosity about the mysterious woman.

CHAPTER 4

*M*ike got up in the middle of the night days later to check the computer availability. Sure enough, most of the camp was asleep with guards stationed at various points to make sure they were safe as they rested. He found that if he befriended the guards, they generally left him alone, but if he snuck around, then he would end up in trouble every single time.

"Computer again, Coop?"

"You know I'm addicted to my game," Mike confessed lightly and opened the door to the building. Sure enough, it was empty at this hour. He was supposed to be sleeping but he couldn't get Cora's email out of his mind and the little necklace he'd purchased seemed to be calling to him. He really wanted to impress Cora and the more he replayed her email, the more he craved contact with her.

Sitting down, he logged in to his game and collected the daily token gift for simply showing up. He wasn't sure how long he would have and knew from experience that other guys snuck into the building at all hours simply for a chance to reach out to their loved ones as well. Mike sent several more candies and tokens to Cora before exiting the game. This surprised him that he didn't even bother to load a game or play a few. He simply wanted to say hello again.

Logging into his email, Mike deleted the junk mail and saw that Cora hadn't replied yet. He sent off a quick email to Wilkes asking for Ava's address and another email to Ethan Minter to see how he was doing. Last he heard, Minter was going through a rough spot trying to find his way and head over heels in love with a woman he'd met named Daisy. Wilkes was supposed to be returning in less than a week, but he couldn't stand the wait. He wanted to mail the necklace to Cora immediately. Cracking his knuckles, he took a deep breath and began to type.

Dear Cora,

I hope you are resting right now but I know with the time difference it's probably about three in the afternoon and I'm betting you are at work. I've kept replaying your email in my mind and still in shock at how we both seem to think a lot alike. I downloaded that music group and you are right – they are fantastic.

You shared so much with me that I wanted to be upfront with you too. I'm lonely and infinitely jealous of some of the relationships others have going on around me. Everyone seems to have someone at home or someone they are talking to. Your words struck me when you referred to wanting a life like a Hallmark movie - now hear me out...

What if we are supposed to be pen-pals? What if this is all some big design by the Big Guy for us to meet someday? I mean, I don't want things to get weird but you seem super nice. What if we are destined to be friends in order to make that next step in our lives?

There are so many thoughts rolling around in my mind right now that I'm a little freaked out, so I can only imagine how you are probably feeling reading this. I'm not some weird stalker – and you are literally thousands of miles from here – but what if we upgraded from friends to 'best-of-friends'? I mean, is there a difference really between the two? I'm being truthful - I'd like more out of this but I can't define what 'that' is right now. It's just my gut instinct is waving the green 'Go!' flag at me.

Sorry I'm rambling. It's just after two in the morning here and I'm probably not thinking straight. I just really enjoyed your emails and wish that I could get the computer more than what I can now. I wish I could email you every day and vice-versa but I know you are busy or scared.

Write when you can,
Mike

RETURNING FROM PATROLS, Mike yanked off his pack and helmet once he got close to the quarters. He was covered in sweat and grit from being out in the sandy, blistering heat. They'd found several homemade bombs and were able to detonate them safely. His ears were ringing from the noise and every time one went off, he expected to hear someone screaming. He still heard it in his sleep sometimes. Untucking his shirt to try and cool off, he stomped his boots onto the ground outside the tents before ducking inside. Walking over to his bunk, he started in surprise at the small package on his bunk.

"You get something, Coop?" Post asked, smirking as he dumped his own gear onto the footlocker at the end of his bunk.

"It's probably yours and you know it, knucklehead," Mike smarted and picked up the box, glancing at it.

"Trust me – that isn't from Annabelle," Post smarted off angrily, causing Mike to look from the package to the other man in surprise.

"What happened? Is planning for the wedding getting to be too expensive?"

"We aren't getting married."

"What? Since when?"

"Since she is pregnant with another man."

"You have got to be kidding me," Mike gaped in shock. Post and his fiancée had been engaged for almost two years. She was the reason he'd signed up for this location voluntarily. He wanted the hazardous duty pay that came with being assigned to Afghanistan. They were saving up for a house and to pay for some huge glorious wedding that Annabelle insisted on.

"Nope. Turns out she hasn't been spending the money on the wedding, she's been living the high-life with some other guy."

"Seriously? Annabelle? I can't see that in her from what you've said about her in the past. She seemed so nice and sweet."

"She is," Post interrupted. "She's so nice, sweet, pretty, and apparently in love with another man. She's pregnant, Mike. I can't marry her after she's strung me along and then fallen for another guy. I broke it off and closed our shared account."

"Post, man, I am so sorry."

"Me too," Post admitted, shaking his head in disbelief. "I'm just really glad that I found out before we got married rather than after. I still care for her and she'll always be special – but to someone else now… not this fool. What did you get, Coop?"

Mike looked down at the box in his hand and felt his heart turn over his chest. It was from Cora. He'd received a few short emails from her, but nothing like the first couple that she'd sent to him. He was simply glad to hear back from her because he was pretty positive he'd scared her off by sharing what he'd thought or felt deep down inside.

It was utterly insane to like someone so much based off a few things they'd said, which made him feel like a gullible fool. There was no way he could be as lucky as Wilkes or Griffin… Post was proof that you just never knew what was going on with someone you cared for. Mike had thought that the couple was untouchable – yet she found someone else.

Unwrapping the paper, he was careful not to tear the return address. He felt himself smile as he saw the P.O. box number, knowing that was another safety measure that Cora took to hideaway. She really didn't trust many people, which made him feel so much more humbled when it came to what she'd shared with him. He would be mailing out the necklace he'd bought her immediately. Wilkes was supposed to be returning any day now but failed to give him an address because he was so busy talking about how much he adored Ava.

Glancing down, at the box in his hands, he laughed. Inside was a single large box of Candy Crush gummy candies. He smiled at the gesture as he opened it up. It was full of little sour squishy candies in the shape of the tokens and candy bombs from the game. Some were melted or stuck together from the heat, but for the most part they were in great condition. Mike happily popped a sour candy in his mouth and grinned at Post who stared at him like he'd lost his mind.

"You must really like gummy candy."

"It's kinda our thing right now."

"You have a thing with her?"

"I certainly do on my end and I'm wondering if she does too."

"Cause she sent you cheap candy?"

"Because she thought enough to send something and I

have her address now to send her a little something in return."

"That makes you weird and a true goofball."

"I'm okay with that," Mike shrugged and tossed another piece of candy up in the air, catching it in his mouth. The burst of sweetness combined with tart powder made him almost gleeful as he realized that Cora might be just like the candy she'd sent. Bitter and sour on the outside, but once you got to the center of who she was, she'd be sweet and utterly wonderful.

THAT EVENING, Mike set an alarm on his watch and got up about three in the morning in order to try to use the computer. He heard his alarm go off and immediately hit snooze, hearing several angry grumbles nearby. He ducked as Post threw his pillow across the room and uttered a few blasphemies. Wilkes was back and hadn't said a word, but collapsed in his bunk at some point after Mike had gone to sleep. The man was lying there fully clothed on top of his covers and snoring from exhaustion. Slipping on his clothing, Mike practically jogged over to the building and took his spot at the empty computer.

CORA,

I can't talk long as I've got to get some rest. It's three in the morning here and I figured the longer I waited, the more likely the computer would be empty. I mailed you something today once I received your package. The candy was completely unexpected and amazing. I can't thank you enough for thinking of me. You didn't have to but it meant a lot to receive something in the mail.

Speaking of, I'm glad you are still emailing but I worry about having said something wrong. You seem to be pulling away and I don't want to drive you off. I really look forward to your emails and it's killing me wondering what I did. You can say anything – and I hope you know that. If you want to tell me to get lost, then say it. I'd rather have the email so I can figure out how to fix things than to deal with the distant politeness. I hope that makes sense.

Mike

MIKE LOADED up the game and sent Cora several more tokens. He clicked back on his email and was stunned to see a response already. A feeling of dread filled him. Cora had never replied so fast – ever. Swallowing hard, he clicked on the notification.

MIKE,

I'm glad you got the candies and enjoyed them. It was really nothing much so I wouldn't make such a big deal about it. Yes, we are friends but you are coming on a little strong for me. You didn't have to send anything in return. That's not necessary. I picked it up because I was grateful for your email and the help you gave me in the game. I get the impression that you are looking for more than a friendship and I told you I have trust issues... lots of them.

I like how you reach out and its flattering that you feel like you can confide in me. I know I really spilled my guts when I wrote you and maybe I gave you the wrong impression. I like you – you seem really wonderful, but I've got to take care of me first because no one else will. Now, if that seems harsh – I'm sorry.

I don't mean to hurt your feelings but I cannot put all my hopes and dreams for more in my life on just your emails... when I barely know who you are. We like the same game, we enjoy similar music, but WE don't KNOW each other and I don't see how we could ever get to know each other on opposite sides of the world. That isn't going to change.

I am here.

You are there.

Distance is my safety net and I need one.

Of course, I write you, Mike – getting your emails is the highlight of my day but I cannot give you more without sacrificing some of who I am. I won't hurt myself mentally or emotionally on a long-distance friendship. Ever hear the term, 'all in on a sure thing'? That's me.

I treasure your emails, your friendship, but as we are practically strangers... that is all we can be, Mike. Please don't be mad or upset.

Cora

MIKE YANKED the trashcan out from under the printer and promptly threw up from the rush of nausea in his body. He was falling for a stranger simply based off of her words and she effectively was shutting him down. He read and re-read her email, feeling his chest sink with each word that she'd typed. It hurt, even if it was the truth.

He had to find a way to bridge the gap between them because she was effectively telling him to back off as a protective measure. She was afraid of being hurt, in her words, mentally and emotionally – which meant he'd reached her in some fashion and she was scared. Hitting reply, he felt himself break out in a cold sweat and sour bile rumbled in his stomach once again from anxiety.

CORA,

I'm not mad and I understand. I value your friendship so much and will give you as much space as you need – just don't run away.

I'll back off.
Mike

CORA STARED through blurry eyes at her cell phone as she sat in the breakroom alone. Ava was working through lunch today to get a bit of overtime on her next paycheck. She was glad to be by herself so no one could see the strangling panic she felt in sending the email - even if it was the truth.

Mike scared her to death because she felt herself reaching out towards him so easily via email. This wasn't normal, and she was terrified of wanting more or being let down again. The emails he sent were so sweet and tender. It was like he wanted to make her smile or was trying to impress her – and he had.

She was growing infatuated with a stranger she'd never met and that was about as terrifying as the clown from the horror movie trailers she'd seen on television. *Letting him down would be better for them both in the long run, wouldn't it?* she wondered, wiping her eyes on a folded paper towel she'd fished out of her lunchbox. If it was better... why did it hurt so much?

OCTOBER 2016

MIKE STARED AT COLIN, feeling his gut clench with jealously at watching how happy his friend was getting the video via email. He'd been exchanging emails with Ethan Minter and John Griffin several times over the last few months in order to prevent himself from doing more damage to the fragile relationship he was trying to nurture with Cora. He was still sending her game tokens and limited his emails to once a week. He would spill out his guts but before clicking send – he would edit the email, removing all emotion from it.

"We both love you so much, Colin. Come home soon!" Mike heard from the iPad that Colin held in his hand. The man sighed heavily as the video ended and looked around, meeting Mike's eyes.

"She's really something, huh?" Mike asked painfully. He was really struggling with keeping from saying anything to her. The last email he had from Cora said that she'd received the necklace from him – and that was it.

"I can't believe how beautiful she is inside and out. She's everything to me."

"You are really lucky," Mike confessed.

"Did you ever email that girl Ava recommended?"

"Yeah."

"Nothing?"

"I guess not every little email will end in sunshine and rainbows, will it?" Mike snapped angrily, feeling a wave of loss roll through him. "Truthfully, I've never met anyone so infuriating in all my life. I mean, I sit there and pour out my guts – only to get head-butted verbally in return."

"Are you serious?"

"Yeah. I guess you and Griffin got the good ones."

"Coop- you know there is someone out there for you too. Maybe you can meet a nice girl when you go on vacation or something."

"You know why I like that game?" he said, pointing at the iPad in Colin's hand. "Because it doesn't demand anything from me and doesn't care whether I play or not. Girls are just too demanding and hard to understand," Mike said, crossing his arms, irritated.

"You know, not to sound crass – but women are like

games. They don't *like* games; they are *similar* to one though. You have to know when to wait your turn, when to step forward, when to put down your cards on the table, and when to cash out and run like crazy. If writing Cora is making your gut instincts scream for you to cash out and run... Do it, buddy. There's bound to be another girl."

Mike laid down in his bunk and stared at the ceiling above him. He laced his fingers behind his head and whispered aloud something he'd never expected to admit to anyone. He was falling for the woman and it was like dying on the inside.

"Not like Cora."

CHAPTER 5

"*I*'m not so sure this is what I need or want anymore," Cora said gently to the young woman sitting behind the desk. Daisy Greenwell was such a kind, gentle person and Cora had really thought that these group meetings would help her come out of her shell. She knew she was afraid to trust anyone or let anyone inside her inner circle.

"Cora, you seem to be coming along so well."

"And you've got some people that need a bit more help than me. I have trust issues and that isn't such a bad thing sometimes."

"No, that is true – but you aren't an island. You are going to need someone in your life someday. How will you handle it? Will you be able to let that person be themselves and can you cope with the fact that you cannot control them? People are bound to make mistakes and let you down at some point – but that doesn't make all of them terrible or unworthy of your friendship or trust."

"I'm trying to make friends."

"How have you changed?"

"Well, for starters – I meet Ava for lunch almost every day and we sit together."

"That's wonderful," Daisy said emphatically, smiling. "Do you have conversations? What do you talk about?"

Cora was surprised by the line of questions. She and Ava rarely talked. At her silence, Daisy nodded knowingly.

"You are going to have to try to make an effort to be part of a group. Sitting with Ava is the first step but you should try chatting with her. Why don't you meet up after work or something? Go shopping or go for a walk in the park. In fact, you could take my newest dog home with you. It would give you an excuse to go for a walk in the park so you felt like you had a purpose in being there. A little distraction can help things along."

"I can't really take a dog," Cora said frowning. "I've got a little place and I'm not much of a dog-person. I mean, I've always wondered what it would be like but not right now."

"Do you even want to meet Dino? He's super sweet and gentle."

"No," Cora said firmly, thinking about her deadlines she needed to hit. Her time was over and now Daisy was on her time. "I appreciate it, but I need to be going. I'll think about what you've said."

"Did you want to schedule again?"

"Not right now," Cora said evasively, "My schedule is hectic and I need to see how everything is going to work out." Daisy nodded knowingly, making Cora fidget nervously at the keen stare from the woman's piercing eyes.

"I'm here if you need to talk."

CORA THOUGHT about Daisy's words over and over again the next several days. Her life had become quite dull, throwing herself into her work all the time with not a lot to show for it. She wanted something new, exciting, and wonderful. The only thing that had fit those qualifications had been receiving Mike's emails. Each time she saw his name pop up in her email, she couldn't help the thrill of happiness that hit her.

"How's your game going?" Ava said congenially at lunch one day.

"Pretty good."

"How's Cooper?"

"Fine."

"You are chock-full of info, aren't you?" Ava announced teasingly.

"I really don't have much to share."

"Don't have – or you don't want to?"

"Maybe both?"

"What are you doing for Thanksgiving, Cora? Do you have family nearby?"

"Me?"

"Yes, you," Ava smiled pleasantly. "I was invited by a few friends to attend a pre-Thanksgiving feast at Shamrock where Daisy Greenwell lives. I guess she's going to be hosting it. There's supposed to be a turkey and all the trimmings."

"Well... I..."

"It's okay if you have plans," Ava said politely. "I just thought I would invite you if you were going to be alone. I hate being alone lately and I seem to be moping quite a bit. I thought getting together with friends might help ease some of the pain in Colin being gone."

"I'm sure it's terrible to say goodbye to him," Cora said sympathetically and suddenly stopped, thinking. Was this what Daisy meant when she said she needed to meet people or talk to them?

"I don't have any plans."

"Then you'll come?"

"Sure. I've got nothing else going on right now."

CHAPTER 6

*N*ovember 2016

CORA SAT GINGERLY in the room and watched the scene unfold in front of her. She'd felt leery about spending the day with everyone for Thanksgiving and now that gut reaction was right. She was so happy for Ava and Colin but no one had ever indicated that Mike Cooper would be flying in with Colin for the holiday.

She'd watched as the tall blond man walked in the front door and Ava practically tackled him like a professional football player. Another man walked in and Cora nearly swallowed her tongue. He was utterly gorgeous. He was almost as tall as Colin with short dark brown hair that looked almost black in the dim lighting and dark eyes that matched. He had a wide enchanting smile that seemed to light up the room and made her heart flutter... and then she heard Colin speak.

"Jeez Coop, gimme a minute or two- will ya?" Colin

groaned in annoyance as he held Ava in a massive bear-hug in the middle of the living room of Daisy's home.

"It's nice to meet you Mr. Cooper," Ava laughed, not letting go of Colin. "No hugs for you, sir. I can't let go of this guy yet."

"You'll never have to," Colin murmured sweetly, making Cora feel envious of the relationship between the two of them.

"Can we get out of the doorway at least?" Mike said ruefully. "It's chilly out compared to Afghanistan. My bum's got goosebumps!" He brazenly reached behind him and rubbed his derriere emphatically against the cool air outside.

A few more introductions and greetings were made before Ava returned to her seat looking stunned. Colin's parents had flown in to see him and it was obvious Ava had no idea what was going on. Cora watched the scene unfold around her, utterly torn. She knew that coming today took her away from much needed time to work. Now she was face-to-face with the man that irritated the fire out of her and scared her like no other could.

Mike.

Ava had told her the man was lonely and wanting a pen-pal. She claimed he was an expert on the game she'd been playing on her cell phone during lunch one day. Even Daisy seemed to be pushing her towards reaching out to someone so she was a part of the world around her and found a way to unwind, relinquishing control. She couldn't help the stringent morals that she'd had to develop to get by. No one else would ever take care of her and she had been alone since she was fifteen – abandoned.

Now, this man wouldn't leave her alone and she'd regretted the initial email. She'd written him, saying hello and confessing about her deepest darkest secrets. There had been no chance that anything would come of it and it was cathartic to get it out on 'paper' it seemed. Only, Mike had written back – with an understanding and offer of friendship that scared her.

And he had never stopped writing even if he'd toned it down a bit!

For every few letters he'd send, she would respond with just a quick note out of guilt. The man was pouring out his guts to her and she felt like an absolute heel. An entanglement meant distractions... distractions meant loss of production – which lead to loss of income.

Cora would never be homeless again.

Ever.

She didn't understand it – and Mike confused her to no end. She liked order, craved it, needed it, in her life. Control kept her safe – and safe kept her fed. Mike was just going to disrupt her life- in more ways than one! She liked him and she couldn't afford the distraction nor the emotional entanglement. It was only a matter of time before the handsome man realized that she was his absentee pen-pal.

Cora wished the floor would just open up and swallow her whole right about now. She even contemplated putting her finger down her throat to get sick so she could run to the car and leave. Desperation and fear were swamping at her emotions. She couldn't meet Mike right now. He just couldn't be this wonderful in his emails and this breathtaking in real life. That was an unfair combo – a one/two punch to the gut. What if he thought she was ugly? What if he wasn't interested but she fell for him? She was practically there already mentally but still had wiggle room to justify the ridiculousness of it all, simply telling herself he was on the opposite side of the planet.

Not. Any. More.

He was right here, in the flesh.

The gorgeous, tanned, sexy flesh that was smiling at her.

Ohmygosh! Cora thought in sheer panic and jumped to her feet.

"I'll be right back," she yelped and ran from the room, locking herself in the bathroom down the long hallway. She stared panicked at the wide-eyed woman looking back at her. Her face was pale with fear of the unknown or feeling of impending doom. Mike was here! Grabbing a washcloth, she heard Daisy's soft voice asking if she was okay as it was followed by a light knocking.

"Cora?"

"You didn't tell me *he* was going to be here!" Cora whispered hotly.

"*He* has a name," she heard a deep, masculine voice nearby that made her bones feel like jelly. "Come on out, Cora, so I can say hello."

"I don't think so."

"I'm not the boogeyman. I'm your friend."

"My friends don't look that hot," Cora chirped and slapped her hands over her mouth in dismay as she heard a deep throaty chuckle.

"This is obviously more than what she's shared with me. Don't run her off, Mike. Give her some space," Daisy's voice carried, followed quickly by Ethan and John urging her away from the door.

"Go away," Cora instructed.

"Nope."

"Well I'm not coming out."

"I've got all night."

"This isn't a contest."

"Nope, this is me trying to say hello."

"Well you said it – now go."

"Cora, be realistic please. Is it so hard to believe that the first person I would want to say hello to is you?"

"Yes – you are surrounded by your friends."

"And you are one of them."

"You aren't going to let up, are you?"

"I don't plan on it – no."

"The bathroom is comfortable, you know. I could hide in here for hours."

"...And I don't have to pee in a toilet."

"Whaaaat?"

"I'm just saying. I'm a guy and I could go find a bush or..."

Cora jerked open the door horrified and stared up at him in disgust. He was standing there with his arms crossed against his chest. His dark eyes sparkled with delight as he smiled.

"You are crass and utterly gross."

"I said it to get a reaction out of you other than being afraid of me."

"Well you got one."

"Great."

"Now, go away."

"I'm here in Texas until almost New Year's Eve."

"Well then I will..."

Cora nearly collapsed in shock as her words were suddenly cut off by Mike. He grabbed her by the shoulders and kissed her. His warm lips pressed against hers and she couldn't help her body's traitorous reaction to him. Her fingers tentatively touched his side, making him giggle against her lips, effectively breaking the kiss.

"I'm ticklish," he whispered softly to her. Cora's eyes flew open and stared at his inky ones just before the catcalls started from nearby. Glancing over, she saw everyone was standing clustered at the end of the hallway. Their faces were lit with knowing smiles and several incorrigible winks.

Backing away, Cora nearly fell into the bathroom doorway behind her but Mike caught her once again. She stood up and abruptly stomped on his foot, jerking her arm away from him. She walked up to the stunned gathering that was blocking her exit.

"Move please."

Thankfully they parted and let her out because Cora felt mortified at having hurt Mike's foot. She didn't like the idea of an audience seeing her first kiss ever from a guy, nor did she want any of them to know it – especially Mike. He was pushy enough as it was without giving him any encouragement.

"Cora! Please don't leave," Daisy said quickly and Ava chimed in.

"Mike Cooper I told you to be on your best behavior with her!"

"I am! I swear it!"

"That wasn't it!"

"Well she isn't scared of me right now."

"No, *she's* mad," Cora announced loudly, making everyone turn and look at her. "... and a little embarrassed by all of this."

"I can handle both of those emotions – just not your fear," Mike said, coming out of the hallway. "Now, would you like something to drink."

"I don't drink."

"I do – Ethan! Do you have any Diet Dr. Pepper? Cora doesn't drink fluids at all..."

"I never said that!" Cora protested immediately. "Don't twist my words."

"Don't look for the worst in me all the time. I was trying to be nice."

"Guys! I just got engaged!" Ava snapped, irritated. "Can you please do this on your own time, not when I want to celebrate with Colin and meet his family officially? I want everyone to spend the day with us *happy* – get it? *Happy* Thanksgiving?"

Cora sat down hard in a chair and felt almost chastised that she had to be told to calm down. Glancing up, she saw Mike looked away from her and disappeared into another room. Everyone seemed to finally spread out amongst themselves.

John Griffin, their former CPO from Afghanistan, was cuddling with his wife Lily nearby, whispering to her. Whatever he was saying had her smiling and blushing. Ethan had found his way towards Daisy's side, his hand gently laying on her hip while congratulating Ava and Colin on their engagement. The two were engaged but had delayed their marriage for a bit for personal reasons. Ava's daughter, Aurora let out a loud shriek of happiness followed by a sweet little giggle that made everyone turn and look at the baby in the older couple's lap where they sat on the couch.

Everyone had someone – except Cora. She'd never felt more alone at this point. The only person remotely interested and got under her skin like no other, was currently missing. Clenching her hands together, she fought the urge to pick up her purse and simply leave. Doing that wouldn't change the way she felt right now but it would enable her to finish up that website she'd been working on. She had nothing else going for her in her life and it had never hurt so much as it did right now.

A laden plate suddenly appeared in front of her face. It was about three inches from her nose, causing her to jerk backwards visibly. One wrong move and she would have pimento on her face. Glancing up, she glared at Mike.

"What are you doing?"

"Trying to start over," he said lightly, taking a seat next to her. He was holding the large plate laden with two of each different appetizer that had been set out on the counter of the kitchen. He was also holding two cans of Diet. Dr. Pepper.

"Would you like one?"

Sighing, Cora accepted the can and murmured her thanks. Why was he trying so hard and why couldn't he simply get the idea that she wasn't interested? *And why are you lying to yourself?* her mind chimed in quickly, making her blush.

"The brownie bites are really good. I think there is cream cheese in the center of them," Mike said casually as he held out the plate again to her. Rolling her eyes, she picked up one and popped it in her mouth. If her mouth was full, she didn't have to talk to him.

It was Thanksgiving and she could cheerfully gorge herself without question. This would prevent her from getting to know him or falling for him. *Gosh, he was beautiful,* she thought, practically sighing as the sweet chocolaty goodness exploded on her tongue in a sensory overload... kinda like his kiss.

"Stop it," Cora muttered with her mouth full, sending a piece of brownie flying from her lips. "Sorry."

"Excuse me?"

"Oh," Cora flushed with embarrassment. "I was talking to myself."

"I do that sometimes," Mike admitted, smiling, "As long as you don't hold a full-on conversation, I'm told that's normal."

"I bet you have big ol' discussions with yourself all the time," she chided and realized that she was teasing him instead of snapping at him. He must have realized it too because his dark eyes practically twinkled as he grinned, revealing a dimple on one of his cheeks.

"I like it when you smile," Mike said quietly, suddenly looking shy. Cora felt her heart thump nervously and a flutter of panic well up. "I'm glad I got the chance to meet my friend on the other end of the computer. I don't want you to regret writing me and I will try hard to keep things easy. If you are feeling nervous, it's okay because I feel like I've got a runaway bullet train charging through my veins right now."

"You do?" she whispered painfully, meeting his eyes.

"Oh yeah," he admitted, rubbing the back of his head nervously. "I've already screwed this up a few times with you. I want to impress you, and messing it up royally."

Stunned by the admission, her eyes watched him carefully looking for any signs of a lie. She knew what she was doing and couldn't help herself. She ultimately felt like she'd been fooled once or twice in her life and was a terrible judge of character. She was afraid she was going to make a mistake again that could be detrimental to herself. As she looked at him, she saw there was no guise, no attempt to coerce her into anything – it was a painfully honest admission from a genuine person.

"Screwed up sounds so harsh," she said suddenly, surprising herself. "Maybe we can just say *'overly enthusiastic and a little on the aggressive side'*. I'd rather you ask me or tell me if you are going to kiss me."

"I like that," he said shyly, "I promise, next time I will ask permission."

"Thank you."

"Was it so terrible?"

"No," she confessed, feeling her face flush with embarrassment.

"Cora," Mike said thickly, leaning towards her. She backed away almost immediately and glared at him, causing him to smile. "I was just going to tell you something – a secret."

Nodding, she sat there on edge as he leaned in towards her ear. She felt his breath against her hair and thought she'd fly off the seat in an adrenaline rush of panic. Instead, she held still as her curiosity was piqued at the supposed secret.

"You are the most beautiful person I've ever seen," he

whispered reverently against the shell of her ear, making her shiver. "I'm sorry about the kiss but I couldn't help myself."

Cora pulled away slightly, but only enough to look at him where he was leaning close to her. His face was only inches away and she was immobile at the unfettered interest she saw in his eyes. What was it about this man?

"Mike, it was my first kiss – *our* first kiss - and it should have been special, not in a bathroom doorway."

"Cora?"

"Yes?"

"You shouldn't have said that. I'm so gonna kiss you again now," he whispered intensely, his dark eyes holding hers.

In a panic, she picked up something off the plate and shoved it directly into his mouth. It was a large table cracker piled high with port wine cheese. The mulberry and bright orange of the cheese smeared on his lips and part of his nose. Instead of being upset, Mike simply cracked up laughing and backed away from her. He shoved the remainder of the cracker in his mouth and grabbed a napkin to clean his face, handing her one for where her finger was covered in cheese.

"You're lucky it was a cracker this time, Coop," Griffin guffawed from across the room. "Last time I broke your nose and my finger." Everyone started laughing at the revelation, with several confused looks between those that didn't know what John was talking about.

"You kissed *John*?"

"In Afghanistan several years ago. I was teasing him about Lily's letters and did it on the cheek. He completely freaked out."

"Apparently you do that to a lot of people."

"Honey - I'm a lover not a fighter," Mike teased good-naturedly bringing on another round of smiles and laughs. He winked at Cora and said affectionately. "You won this round but the war has just begun."

CHAPTER 7

*C*ora was stunned by the intensity of the way Mike was pursuing her. There was no other way to describe it. Every time she turned around on Thanksgiving – he was there. He was ingenious about it as well, getting past her defenses. Instead of asking for her phone number, he claimed his new phone wasn't working or picking up signal. Loving technology as much as she did, she instantly went to work looking at his phone, checking the settings and testing it with hers.

"It seems to be working okay."

"I see that now. Thank you."

Glancing down at the phone he retrieved from her, she saw him save her phone number immediately with a large smile on his face.

"You little sneak," she breathed, impressed by how clever he'd been.

"I couldn't have gotten it any other way, could I?"

"No, probably not," she admitted, feeling herself smile.

There was something about him that made her instantly leery and she realized what it was now. He could read her probably better than she could read herself. He knew she was wary but he wouldn't give up either. When he claimed that she'd won the battle, she foolishly thought that he was going to give it a rest for a bit, but that wasn't the case. He was mingling around the room, chatting with everyone, but kept returning to her. It was flattering to see him being so attentive towards her. She didn't even have to try; he was just there – for hours on end. At the end of the evening, he walked her to her car and stood there awkwardly beside her waiting in the dim glow of the streetlight.

"You can head back inside."

"I know."

"Aren't you cold?"

"Yeah."

"Then go on inside."

"I'll wait."

"For what?"

"For you to ask me to kiss you."

"No, Mike – I said you should ask me."

"Okay. Cora, may I kiss you goodnight?"

"No."

"See it doesn't work," he said in a disappointed voice. "Maybe I'm saying it wrong? How should I ask?"

"Just say something simple like *'will you please kiss me'*?"

Cora saw the smile on his face and realized what she'd just said aloud.

"You sneaky thing…" she started as he stepped forward. She backed up and bumped into her car. His arms slid around her waist, and he simply waited, smiling down at her.

"You are right. That was sneaky," he admitted softly, kissing the tip of her nose. "Will you please let me kiss you? We aren't in a bathroom doorway, and there is no one around. It's just you and me – and I want to make our first kiss a little better than that rushed one. You can even stomp on my foot again," he offered, making her melt a little.

"Maybe just a little kiss," she conceded, wondering what a true kiss would be like from him if just seeing his smile made her feel giddy inside. He leaned down and hesitated again, his warm breath mingling with hers in the cool night air.

"Last chance, honey," he breathed, "No take-backs now."

Nodding, she closed her eyes and heard his breath hitch just before his lips touched hers tenderly. She felt herself melt into his arms as his hand slid up and cupped her cheek, the other arm holding her close to him. Cora reached out to put her arms around his waist and the second she made contact, he giggled again. She laughed in delight against his lips.

"You really are ticklish, aren't you?"

"Horribly so," he admitted, smiling down at her. "Just go ahead and put your hands on my waist. Don't be shy, that is what tickles. Grab me like you are picking up something off the floor."

"Mike," Cora said in amazement, chuckling. "Kissing you shouldn't be like picking up something on the ground."

"I'm glad you think that way," he confessed, winking at her mischievously. "Go ahead and place your hands on me. I wasn't done in the slightest."

"So, if it's too much, all I have to do is tickle you?"

"Sure," he snickered, as she put her hands on his waist quickly. She felt the skin under his shirt clench under her fingers and nearly moaned aloud at the sensation it created inside of her. He was nothing but muscle under her finger-tips as he settled in under her touch.

"Now, where were we?"

"You were trying to right a wrong – weren't you?" she said boldly, reminding him of the impromptu kiss earlier that was so unexpected. This would be an afternoon she would never forget. Her world was in the process of turning upside down and it centered around this endearing, lonely soldier.

"Yeah, I was."

THE NEXT SEVERAL days were a bevy of text messages and phone calls just to check to see what she was up to. Mike was a massive distraction in her life – a pleasant one. Cora was invited over to dinner by Mike under the premise that everyone else was going to be there. He must have realized she was going to hesitate because he quickly volunteered the information over the phone. As she listened to him speak, she realized that he was telling the truth.

"Apparently, everyone is gathering together at a restaurant in town this evening about six tonight. Do you want me to pick you up? I could borrow Ethan's truck," he offered.

"No, I can drive myself."

"Somehow I knew you'd say that."

"Why?"

"Because I know you don't want anyone to know where you live."

"How do you know that?"

"You haven't told me plus you use a P.O. box. I know you value your privacy."

"My place is just a little apartment and there is no reason to come over."

"Other than to get to know you a little better."

"Mike, there isn't much to it."

"But it's yours, right?"

"Well, yeah?"

"Then I'd be happy to see it."

"You're a dork, you know that?"

"I'm *your* dork, sweetheart," he said tenderly before ending the call. Cora smiled at the phone in her hand and felt her heart sing in happiness. Yeah he was, she thought happily and tried to ignore the nagging fear in her. Everything seemed to be going so smoothly and she kept waiting for the problems to creep up between them.

Finishing up, Cora got ready and quickly headed out to the dinner at the Mexican restaurant that everyone was meeting at. Pulling up, she saw several cars in the parking lot, a lot more than what she'd expected. Walking inside, she realized that the back corner of the restaurant had the tables reserved for them and was corded off from the others. Seeing Mike flag her down, she walked over immediately and walked around the chair that was blocking the way.

"What's going on?"

"Colin and Ava have an announcement, I think," he whispered, sneaking a quick kiss on her cheek that made her do a double take. "Sorry."

"It's okay," she breathed, nodding quickly. Taking a seat, she quickly ordered unsweet tea and saw Mike ordered the same but asked for a plate of limes too. She arched an eyebrow in surprise.

"What? I like a little something tart in my life," he teased lightly. "You should try it."

"Maybe I will."

Several more people came to sit down at the tables around them as the waiters brought out several bowls of queso, guacamole, and chips. The gathering group was making introductions and several hugs. Mike jumped to his feet and grinned, embracing another man in a huge bear hug. Cora watched in curiosity until Mike turned and immediately introduced her.

"Jamie Post, this is my lovely girl. Cora, Jamie is one of

my best friends back in Afghanistan. Man, I thought you were going home for the holiday?"

"A lot has changed and I got an email I couldn't refuse at the last minute."

"What's that?"

"My cue," Colin interrupted, hugging Jamie. It brought tears to Cora's eyes as Ethan and John came over as well. The group was obviously very close, almost as if they were family. They had each other and were cutting up in a friendly banter that made her envious. Ava seemed to sense what was going through Cora's head and stepped around the group to talk to her.

"They really are something, aren't they?"

"Apparently the best of friends."

"They've all been through a lot," Ava said knowingly, smiling at where Colin stood. "I know what you are thinking right now cause I felt that way too."

"What?"

"You feel like a spectator, an intruder on this moment," she admitted sagely, smiling at Cora. "Trust me, you aren't. The moment we became friends, you became part of our extended family. Mike would have my hide if you felt worried or that you needed to leave."

"Why do you say that?"

"Because he told me to be on my best behavior," Ava confided, "In fact, his exact words were *don't screw this up for me, guys*. He really likes you."

"He's a bit intense."

"They all are in their own way. Mike's a goofball. He will keep you laughing, according to Colin. Speaking of which, I think he's signaling me. Gotta go!"

Mike quickly took his seat on the bench beside Cora and picked up her hand easily. He laced his fingers with hers and set it on the cushion between them. Looking up at Ava and

Colin, it was easy to see the love between them. He was incredibly loving towards the tiny woman that stood next to him. Ava barely came up to Colin's shoulders but neither cared in the slightest at their differences. It was simply a matter of their personalities just fitting together. Ava could do no wrong in Colin's eyes and it was obvious. Cora sneaked a peek at Mike to see him watching her out of the corner of his eyes. He pursed his lips in a smile and squeezed her hand in a silent response as Ava began to speak.

"We've invited you all here to share with us something special. As you know, we've all been through ups and downs over the last several years that have affected us in one way or another. When I met Colin online, I was in a really rough spot and he's been my guiding light on returning to the person I used to be."

"Honey, I think that is the other way around," Colin interrupted tenderly, wrapping his arms around her waist and looking down at her over her shoulder from where he stood behind her.

"You all have been so much of our lives that we wanted to share the start of our life together with you. This has been a quick decision that was easily made between us as you are all here for the next few weeks. We want to get married in a few weeks and we want you to join us at the wedding." Several whoops, clapping hands, and cries of delight filled the air around them before they all settled down for Ava to speak again.

"Everything seems to be coming together as if designed. The church is free on Saturday, December 10th which gives us a little over a week to throw things together. We've gotten our license and my mama is going to make the cakes for us. I don't have time to get invitations printed and mailed though – which is why I thought this would be ideal to share good food amongst the best of friends and family."

"To Colin and Ava," Ethan said joyously, rising to his feet carefully due to his prosthetic leg. "May you both have plenty of adventure and love for the years to come." Another chorus of applause sounded, almost deafening as this time Colin indicated he wanted to say something.

"Post, Coop, Minter – guys, I want you to stand up with me when I make Ava my bride. No tuxes needed, just wear your uniform and we'll be thrilled."

"You got it, Wilkes," Mike chimed in happily, bringing Cora's hand up and kissing her knuckles. She was surprised at the display of affection in front of everyone as he glanced at her nervously.

"Sorry."

"You don't have to say that," she hedged, feeling guilty about him needing to apologize for it. She saw he looked to be nearly bursting with joy and it was infectious. He was smiling brightly at her reaction and she understood what Ava was saying now. He wanted her to be a part of his world and wanted to make sure she felt welcomed. It was sweet of him to be so very protective of her and made her feel treasured.

"Lily, Daisy, and Cora? Girls, will you stand up with me? We can get some matching dresses at the mall that should work for bridesmaid's gowns. All that is left is to get a few bouquets, have the wedding, and celebrate."

"Let's pick out something pretty for little Aurora first and then we can match our gowns to her color," Cora suggested shyly. Colin and Ava grinned at each other before nodding.

"I love that idea. Thank you."

"All my pretty girls will match," Colin teased.

"Marry your girl, leave mine alone," Mike joked and smiled at Cora.

"Your safe, Mike," Cora quipped easily, feeling comfortable in being a part of the group surrounding them. "I'm not interested in him."

"Just me?"

"We'll have to see about that," she said blandly and winked at Mike to take the sting out of her words. Everyone began to settle in as the servers brought out plates and plates of food served family style. Cora felt like she belonged for the first time in forever.

She'd been alone for so long and never realized the comfort in having someone care for you. Mike was spoiling her – quickly. He kept her drink filled and offered some of his limes for her to try. When the platters came around, he asked if she wanted to try it, and then served it up for her. It was humbling at just how nice he was being simply because he wanted to. She kept waiting and watching, looking to see if there was going to be a problem in them being friends. She didn't even want to consider the label of 'boyfriend' just yet. As they ate, she listened to him talking with Post about the change of plans.

"I thought you were going home for Christmas?"

"Not after what happened, plus I got a better offer."

"Here?"

"Yeah. I couldn't believe it when Wilkes sent me the email. He's lucky I saw it in time. I was getting ready to refund my flight and just hang out at the barracks back home and mope."

"That sounds like an awful idea," Mike retorted. "I'm glad you are here."

"Truthfully, me too. What are you two up to?"

"Nothing really," Mike hedged, looking at Cora uneasily. "I'm trying not to crowd my girl too much. I don't want to barge in on all her free time."

"We haven't made any plans," Cora interrupted. "Did you have any suggestions? Are you from the area?"

"I'm not, but I remembered reading that usually right after Thanksgiving there are holiday shops that open up for the season only. I think you can paint ornaments, decorate cookies, or some other things."

"Would you like to join us?" Cora asked politely, feeling sorry for the man. If they were friends, she wanted Mike to feel like she was trying to include his friends in things while they were in town. She hoped he would accept simply so she wasn't alone with Mike, but a bigger part of her wanted him to decline the offer the moment she'd said it.

"No," both men said immediately, looking at each other in horror.

"Post, I love ya' like a brother – but you are not going out with Cora and I," Mike said possessively. Seeing his reaction to someone tagging along shot a thrill straight up her spine. He wanted her to himself – and she liked it!

"Nor do I want to," Jamie said immediately. "You two need to do your own thing and I will find something to occupy my time. It's sweet that she's nice to your friends, Cooper. Don't be too nice though, Cora. Spend some time together while you can. Maybe you can put up a Christmas tree together or make some cookies."

"I don't put up a tree," Cora said quietly, not wanting to explain why either. It was embarrassing to admit she hadn't bought another one since hers had been stolen by Becca. Mike watched her carefully and nodded quietly. She saw his mind was racing as he was trying to figure out why she didn't celebrate. He quickly squeezed her hand in a silent acknowledgement.

"We'll think of something to do, if she's free for a bit," he said evasively and began to eat his meal again, changing subjects with Post as they talked. As everyone was wrapping up dinner, Mike got up and went to speak with the waiter. He slid back into the table and nodded at Post, who grinned in response. It didn't take long to figure out what the two were up to when Cora suddenly heard Ava's shocked gasp nearby.

"Michael Cooper, you sly dog! You didn't have to do that!"

"What did you do?" Cora whispered, concerned at the dismay written all over Ava and Colin's faces.

"It was Post's idea."

"Don't blame this on me!"

"Fine. It was Cora's idea."

"What?" she screeched. "I don't even know what you did!"

"We paid the bill as a wedding gift to Ava and Colin," he said gently, leaning towards her to tell her quietly what was going on.

"No, we didn't. *You* did."

"*We* did."

"Mike," Cora protested quietly. "How much was it?"

"Don't worry about it."

"I won't take charity."

"...And I don't give it."

"Mike, please. I want to share in the burden. This was a nice meal."

"Cora, relax," he said firmly, kissing her knuckles where her fingers were laced with his. "But if you don't stop arguing and let us both take credit for it then it loses something in the moment. I might have to kiss you again to end the discussion."

"Is that supposed to be a threat?"

"No, sweetheart – it's a promise for later," he said tenderly, tucking a lock of hair behind her ear. "Let me spoil you while I'm here... please."

"You don't have to do that."

"Maybe I want to," he admitted, kissing her on the cheek.

CHAPTER 8

*T*hursday evening had been a mishmash of fabric, laughter, and hugs as they had gone shopping for bridesmaid dresses. Cora had been worried about spending the money but she'd transferred some of her funds from her savings to her checking in order to save face. The computer she was saving for would have to wait a little while longer as the deadline of the upcoming wedding was nearing closer every day.

Aurora seemed to realize that something special was going on because she was in a particularly good mood and cooing sweetly at everyone nearby at the department store. They found a petal pink dress that was covered in little rosebuds for Aurora, prompting the women to find pink dresses to match.

As they peered through the racks, they found a selection of several gowns that were similar in color but different in cut. They took turns trying on the garments while another watched the baby. Apparently Ava already had a dress purchased from a local resale shop that would fit. When she said everything was coming together like it was designed – she meant it.

Cora's gown was a pink sheath dress with fluttery sleeves instead of the spaghetti straps like Daisy was wearing. Daisy's gown looked retro, like it was out of the fifties with a full crinoline skirt that fell below her knees. It was so beautiful you barely realized that the legs peeking out were metallic in nature.

Lily's dress was a bit longer with pleats on the side that were tethered up at her waist, revealing a bit of leg but not indecently in the slightest. The flowing overdress made it look almost wispy or fanciful in nature.

The girls all picked out matching combs for their hair and a large pink bow for Aurora's head. Ava found a pair of knit booties that resembled little ballet slippers for her daughter at the register. Each woman rang up their purchases, chatting amicably until it was Cora's turn. As she fished for her wallet in her purse, Ava stepped forward and handed the cashier a credit card.

"What are you doing?"

"Following instructions," Ava said simply with a secretive smile on her face.

"Mike?"

"He said to spoil you like a princess while we are out today," Ava admitted and Cora felt her face flush with embarrassment as the cashier gushed happily about wishing she had a man who would spoil her.

"Ladies, we are having Ghirardelli's on Mr. Mike Cooper as well," Ava crowed happily. "I'm thinking a little hot fudge sundae sounds like just what we need and I know Colin wants a brownie."

"I don't want to spend all of Mike's money," Cora said hotly, reaching for the credit card as the cashier tried to hand it back to Ava.

"Cora, you realize that Mike has nobody in his life – right? Just you. Colin said he's been putting away his checks for years now because he doesn't have any reason to use it. He lives on base, doesn't drive a car, etc. You are the only thing that has made the big goofball truly happy," Ava advised.

"Let him spend it because I'm telling you now – if he didn't want to? He wouldn't. He's never even bought himself a gadget to play his game on. He has a 'pay by the month' cellphone that he barely uses unless he's in the States."

Cora extended her hand silently towards Ava, who handed her the card with a heavy sigh. She didn't want to feel like Mike was buying her time with him or that she felt obligated to be nice to the guy cause he bought her things. She wanted to be nice to him because of who he was. Mike was in for a rude surprise if he thought he could buy her affection. This was just what Cora had feared – that someone was going to manipulate or use her for their own reasons.

"If you want ice cream, it will be my treat," Cora said simply, smiling. "Besides, a warm caramel sundae with extra whipped cream and cherries sounds perfectly divine right about now."

"I'm still getting Colin his brownie," Ava warned with a smile. Lily nodded towards Daisy before she put her hand on Cora's shoulder gently. Both of them looked at her with a glimmer of respect in their eyes. They understood or at least approved of what she'd said, making her feel a little better about putting her foot down.

"No one wants or expects you to let Mike push his way around. Its good of you to look out for the man, just remember – he wants to watch out for you too. You are among friends and each one of us is very protective about the other. We'd never deliberately cause anyone in our group a problem."

"Maybe Mike will want a brownie," Cora hedged slightly, "But I'm still buying – not him."

"I'm thinking John wants a few chocolate-covered straw-berries and I know Ethan likes those brownies too," Lily replied, nodding emphatically and linking arms with Cora as they headed out into the mall for their treats.

MIKE SURPRISED her by calling and asking her to pick him up at the Wal-Mart in town. Cora had just gotten off of work and had an incredible headache from squinting so long at the computer screen the night before. She was trying to catch up on lost time and staying up late in order to get the jobs in the queue finished on time.

"Do you need a ride?" Cora asked, feeling guilty that she was so short with him. "I'm sorry, my head is killing me."

"Well, kinda," Mike hedged, "Plus you still have my card, according to Ava. I didn't want to bother you Thursday evening when she told me and I figured there was no safer place for it to be right now."

"I'm on my way."

Cora made a U-turn and headed towards the store. She had forgotten about it being in her purse until Ava said something during lunch. Looking in her wallet- she saw the bank card, not a credit card like she'd originally thought. She was glad he wasn't charging stuff left and right – rather he was paying for it outright. Parking her car, she called his cell phone. He didn't answer. Feeling incredibly frustrated, Cora called it again.

"Hello?"

"I'm here."

"Can you come inside the garden center? I want your opinion on something."

"Mike, what are you doing?" she asked annoyed.

"Waiting for you," he replied evasively and she could practically picture the goofy grin on his face. She wondered what he could be up to as she got out of the vehicle.

Cora punched the button to hang up the call and threw her phone in her purse. She didn't have time for him to play his games or be evasive. She wanted to get home, take some Tylenol for her headache and get back to work.

If he bought her a plant, she'd just get a refund immediately. There was no way she was going to attempt to take care of anything like that again. Walking inside, she saw that he had a basket full of things already bagged up and it was filled to the brim.

"Did you buy out the entire store?"

"No, of course not."

"I don't know if I can get all of that in my car."

"Then that's going to be a problem."

"Why?" she asked hesitantly, watching him closely, and saw the cashier was smiling at them.

"Come here, beautiful," he smiled, extending his hand towards her. Cora slipped her hand in his as he suddenly twirled her around happily. The man exuded happiness and she couldn't help the smile that touched her face. "Cover your eyes, sweetheart."

"Mike, what's going on?" she asked, feeling his hands cover her eyes as they began to walk slowly away from the front of the store.

"Trust me, Cora. I won't let you fall or get hurt," he whispered in her ear, "I want to show you something."

"Like what? Where the lawn furniture is displayed?"

"Think bigger."

"The really *big* lawn furniture on display then?"

"Cora – play along with me," he teased, chuckling as he walked her down the aisle against his body to indicate the direction. Coming to a stop, her face pulled against his hands and she stopped moving.

"Can I open my eyes?"

"It depends."

"On what you believe in," he whispered playfully. "Do you believe in magic or fantasy? Or are you more of a traditional kind of girl?"

"What kind of question is that?"

"One you have to answer in order to open your eyes. I'm not pulling my hands away until you confess, even though I think I know who you are deep down inside."

"Oh, you know me, huh?"

"I'd like to think so."

"So, let's hear your theories then, Smarty-pants."

"I think you'd pick traditional every single time because it's safe but deep down inside, in the darkest part of your soul – you believe in magic so wonderful and fragile that its breathtaking to behold," he whispered in her ear and gently kissed her earlobe.

"Am I right, my lovely Cora?"

"Yes," she whispered, entranced and in utter awe at the feelings coursing through her right now. She loved this playful, mysterious side of him and was touched by how right he was. He did know how she thought or how she would react. She felt his hands move from her eyes before they rested on her shoulders. Opening her eyes slowly, she stared at the pale white tinsel tree in front of her that practically glowed with all the lights on it. It was covered in frosted turquoise ornaments that looked like the tree had been snowed on.

"That one?"

"It's lovely."

"Is that the one you'd pick?"

"Pick for what?"

"I want to celebrate Christmas with you and that involves us putting up a tree together, ornaments, baking cookies, and other stuff that couples do... and before you argue with me about it? Yes, we are a couple. We are going to do the boyfriend/girlfriend thing," he said smiling down at her.

"I think you are amazing, incredible, and utterly lovely. I can think of no better way to spend this Saturday than hanging around with you and putting up decorations. Now, having me spill my guts out right here in the middle of Walmart - what do you think?"

Cora watched completely stunned as Mike got down on one knee. Her heart hammered in her chest as she felt herself trying hard to draw air into her lungs. If he proposed, she'd faint dead-out onto this concrete floor! Mike held up a large candy cane pole towards her that he pulled from his pocket and grinned.

"Cora Dillion, will you do me the honor of spending Christmas with me?"

"Get up Mike!"

"It's a yes or no question, honey."

"Mike..."

"Let me try it again in case I made a mistake the first time I said it," Mike said stubbornly, clearing his throat and smiling earnestly as he wiggled the large candy cane at her. They were drawing a crowd and people were getting out their cell phones to video tape the scene they were making in the middle of the garden center.

"My breathtakingly beautiful Cora Dillion, the woman I adore more than the air I breathe, would you do this poor wretched soldier the honor of having Christmas with me? Let's put up a tree together, roast marshmallows, and sing Christmas carols. I will bake you Christmas cookies and rub those pretty little feet..."

"He can come home with me, honey, if you aren't going to say yes!" some woman jeered from the crowd, causing several people to laugh and titter with delight around them. Mike just sat there and wagged his eyebrows mockingly as he waited patiently.

"Yes," Cora answered as a large cheer rose up around them. Mike handed her the cane triumphantly and kissed her on the cheek.

"Good, because I already had them ring this tree up and I'm ready to go. I just need my bankcard, sweetheart."

"What you *need* is your head examined."

"You can feel free to do a thorough physical on me anytime you want," he quipped, winking at her as her face turned bright red at the intimate innuendo he announced so boldly, causing more laughter. She wasn't about to let him have the last word though.

"I might be tempted if you weren't so absolutely ticklish," she smarted. "You fix that problem and maybe I'd be tempted to kiss you more often."

"Challenge accepted, sweetheart."

WITHIN TEN MINUTES, they were unloading the contents of the shopping cart into the trunk of her car. Mike wouldn't let her lift a thing, insisting on picking it all up for her. She stopped him when she saw the large bag of dog food and the twenty-four pack of diet soda.

"Mike, stop! You got someone else's cart!"

"Nope. This is mine," he said lifting the massive bag onto his shoulder and dropping it into the large trunk of her old Buick.

"You have a dog?"

"No, and we need to talk about that."

"What? I don't have a dog. What are we going to talk about?"

"The dog."

"Mike, I can't take care of a dog. I kill plants because of lack of care."

"You'll be fine and Dino is super sweet."

"Dino? As in *the* Dino from group?"

"Daisy said you've already met him a few times. He's the big dog that is part Golden Retriever and who knows what."

"Wait – what? First the tree and now you are getting me a dog? This is my life, not yours, Mike. I don't know if I am responsible enough to maintain taking care of a dog, plus they are expensive. What if he has to go to the vet or gets sick? What if something happens to him and I can't get him help? I can't do this..." Cora whispered, backing away from him. "I can't have you putting responsibility on me that I am not ready for."

"Cora, sweetheart," Mike said gently, gathering her into his arms. She could feel her mind swirling, a mixture of dismay and excitement. She'd always wanted a dog, but was afraid to adopt one. They stood there for several moments in front of the open trunk of her car together, Mike just holding her and kissing her tenderly on the head.

"I know it's hard, honey but just trust me on this. I think a dog would give you something to care for and love. He would protect you and make you feel not quite so worried all the time. I happen to think you are going to be the best doggy-mommy ever," he said gently, smoothing her hair.

"Mike, what if he gets sick when I'm not home."

"Then you'll get him to the vet as soon as you get home."

"The Golden mix is a big dog and I have a little apartment."

"Which I haven't seen yet."

"It's not a great idea to have a big dog in the apartment."

"No, you'll have to walk him a lot or take him to the park."

"I don't have time."

"You should make time for yourself. You have to take care of yourself until I come back and I can pamper you like I'm supposed to."

"You don't have to do any of this."

"I want to," Mike said smoothing back her hair from her face. She looked up at him and was stunned by the raw emotion in his eyes as he looked at her. "I'm only here for a few more weeks and Dino would be something to love you when I am gone."

Cora opened her mouth to say something and he smiled sadly, putting his finger on her lips. He still held her in his arms as if he didn't want this moment to end.

"Don't say anything yet. I probably shouldn't have told you how crazy I am about you, but I can't help myself. Let me earn your trust and your love. Let me be the person you can depend on when you need something. Give me a chance to be everything you need before you say no."

"Is this about the dog?"

"This is about everything between us."

"You are so... so..." she stammered, unsure what to say.

"In love with you?"

"I was going to say *pushy*."

"I'll take that too," he grinned and let out a whoop of laughter as she began to tickle him out of sheer annoyance. His reaction made her giggle as he jumped away from her like he'd been burned.

"Come here you!" he bit out through gritted teeth, trying to keep from laughing as he gathered her in his arms, pinning hers. She was barely able to wiggle her fingers against his side. Cora grinned wickedly as he smiled at her.

"You've got a mischievous streak, don't you?"

"About a mile wide."

"I love it – and I love you," he admitted, kissing her. "Now, let's get this stuff delivered to your place. We have a full day planned for tomorrow that doesn't include tickling at all."

CHAPTER 9

*C*ora spent the entire weekend with Mike. They took hours decorating the Christmas tree he'd selected as well as a variety of plastic ornaments. She laughed at some of the childish things he'd picked up – things she'd not seen since she was a girl. They baked Colorforms and she laughed when he refused to bake the Hulk because he was supposed to be larger than the rest of the team. They also made some stained-glass kits for the holiday and stuck them to the sliding glass door of her little apartment as suncatchers. He never said a thing about her studio apartment.

"Sorry there isn't much to sit on, just the one chair."

"It's nothing, Cora. You are worrying about the small stuff, sweetheart."

"It's kind of a big thing to me."

"Why?"

"One chair, two people," she quipped obnoxiously, smiling at him.

"One wonderful solution," Mike announced mischievously, sweeping her up in his arms and sitting down in the worn-out recliner. Cora was draped across his lap comfortably as they watched Rudolph on the television.

"You really don't mind?"

"This is a perfect afternoon and I'd use any reason to be close to you," he admitted, kissing her forehead, "furniture was just a little bit lower on my list of excuses, but it will definitely do."

They were supposed to go together to pick up Dino from Daisy's house later this evening. She was a little nervous about the dog, but Mike insisted it would be alright. He'd put out a refillable bowl of water, a large puffy dog bed, and a bowl of dog food in order to prepare the home. He also made sure and zip-tied her cords together, encasing them in a plastic protective sleeve, just to be on the safe side. He chatted amicably about how when he was growing up, he'd had a chocolate Labrador that used to chew on furniture. Glancing around her place, she realized there wasn't much that Dino could destroy here. She was heartily impressed that he seemed to think of everything that could possibly go wrong and addressed it in a reasonable manner. Just when she was lost in thought, he suddenly spoke up.

"I promised my girl some Christmas cookies," he taunted playfully, setting them back to work. It was as if he was trying to squeeze as much life as possible into their limited time together. She hated that her work seemed to interrupt her thoughts. She was afraid of getting behind.

"I'd love a few fresh baked cookies. Can I start a pan and check my email to see what's going on?" she hesitated, wondering if he'd get upset. He looked almost apologetic and dismayed.

"Oh Cora, I'm so sorry. I've kept you from your program-ming by insisting we spend time celebrating. Go ahead, honey. I'll make the cookies for us and I'd like to see what it is you can do – if you don't mind showing me?"

"I'd love to – are you sure you don't mind?"

"Not in the slightest."

She started up her computer and waited for it to load. A few minutes later, she walked into the kitchen and microwaved a cup of water to make herself some tea.

"Do you want some hot tea, Mike?"

"I thought you were going to check your mail?"

"I am – it just takes a bit to load. Tea?" she repeated, wincing as she heard the computer fan start to make a squeaking and whirring sound before quieting down. "That's new," she joked, making light of it when his eyebrows shot up in alarm.

"Should you turn it off?"

"Oh gosh no," she immediately argued, "then it will take twice as long. Oh look – there's the screen. I'll be right back." Cora walked over to the table and immediately scanned through her emails. Sure enough, there were two jobs due out today and thankfully they were fairly small in size. She immediately set to work and ignored the noises coming from the kitchen as Mike sliced the roll of sugar cookie dough. Hearing the pan slide into the oven, she glanced up to see him walking to her side. Thankfully, she had two dining room chairs that could be used at the makeshift desk. Mike sat down silently beside her as her fingers flew over the keyboard. After several minutes, he rubbed his eyes and interrupted her train of thought.

"I can't read any of that. The screen is blurry and there's a green spot."

"It's coding."

"It's blurry, Cora – either that or I need glasses."

"Mike, it's not that bad – besides, ol' Bessie has everything I need saved to her hard drive and an external one. I couldn't bear to part with her," she said lamely hiding the fact that she was planning on doing that very thing as soon as she could afford to.

"What if Bessie died a violent hard-drive death?"

"I'd be crushed and my work would be lost – and she is fine. Now, I'm almost finished encrypting this if you'll give me about another ten minutes."

"Take all the time you need," Mike offered and kissed her on the cheek tenderly before he got up. As the timer went off on the microwave, she smelled the warm vanilla scent of the cookies and kept on typing. It wasn't until she realized her neck was hurting that she glanced up to see it was getting dark outside. Turning around, Cora's heart leapt as she saw Mike was sound asleep in the recliner. He'd moved to let her work uninterrupted and occupied himself by watching TV until he'd dozed off. Getting up, she walked over and tenderly kissed him on the lips.

"Wake up, sleeping beauty."

"I don't wanna," he whispered softly. "I was having this amazing dream that you kissed me."

"I did."

"Without tickling me either."

"I know."

"Must be love, huh?" Mike quipped lightly, shutting his eyes again and smiling.

"It just might be," she admitted shyly, feeling strangely relieved to admit the feelings she was having for him. His dark eyes opened and stared up at her silently. Cora sat gingerly on the armrest of the chair and brushed a lock of his hair off his forehead. "I've never met anyone else quite so amazing as you are and it's a little scary to realize that I want to share all of my time with you."

"It shouldn't be scary."

"Only because I set these insane deadlines and have a crazy work schedule."

"Loving someone means accepting them regardless of their crazy work schedule or how far away they are from home."

"I somehow know that," she confessed, "but what am I going to do when you have to leave?"

"If I know you, you'll probably throw yourself into your work to make time fly by, but I'm hoping somewhere in that beautiful mind you'll find time to miss me and wish I was here."

"I will miss you – more that I want to think about."

"Why do you think I push so hard to be with you all the time? Cora, I was half in love with you when I got off the airplane. Seeing how beautiful you are on the outside only heightened my feelings for you."

"What do we do next?"

"We go pick up our Dino and try not to think about what's coming. Let's just enjoy the time we have together while we can. We'll figure something out, sweetheart, but I want to hear it again," he asked tenderly, cupping her cheek.

"What do we do next?" she teased playfully repeating the same sentence again. She felt extremely shy and so very vulnerable right now. It would only take one wrong thing to crush this precious fragile emotion growing in her soul.

"Tell me you love me, sweetheart," he urged, smiling at her response. "Don't ever be concerned to tell me exactly what's on your mind or in your heart. You can tell me I'm a dork all you want, get frustrated with me, or even get angry – but I still want to know I have a spot in your heart at the end of the day."

"I love you, Mike," she breathed softly, staring up into his eyes as he leaned down to kiss her. His lips were infinitely tender and barely grazed hers.

"Perfection."

THE HOURS FLEW by as they met the other couples for dinner. Cora really felt like she was starting to fit into their group. She didn't feel so threatened and truthfully, they expected nothing from her. If she sat there silently or chatted in a conversation, everyone still had a good time. There were no underhanded comments, no sly insinuations – they were upfront honest people. This made her wonder at what kind of company she'd kept before now! She had no idea people could actually be this friendly and not expect something in return. She unfortunately also realized now that growing up she didn't have the best home life having seen her mother be manipulated by others. Nothing would diminish the love she felt for her, but it made her see things a bit more clearly as well.

Dino was another matter.

She didn't understand the dog at all. He literally would stop what he was doing, flop down onto the floor and show his belly. He did it several times at Daisy's house, shocking her each time. The dog would let out a massive *'whoomph'* as he threw himself bodily onto the linoleum flooring.

"Is he alright?" Cora asked warily. "He doesn't have an equilibrium problem or injury – does he? Why in the world does he keep collapsing?" Mike laughed at her question and got down on the ground beside the dog, scratching his belly. The shaggy golden tail swept the floor and his pink tongue hung from his mouth eagerly.

"Cora, have you ever had a dog before?"

"No. I had a bunny when I was much younger and I promise you, Cadbury did not do that. He would kick up his heels if he was in a playful mood."

"When dogs feel secure or want affection, they expose their underside as a show of trust. Dino didn't do this for me the other day," Mike explained, smiling up at her, "He's doing this for your benefit. Come pet him."

She knelt down beside Mike and tentatively reached out a hand only to have the large yellow dog flop over again quickly, alarming her as he began shoving his nose in her hand. Cora flinched as the cool, wet nose left moisture on her palms and fingers.

"Ughh! He snotted all over my hand."

Mike burst out laughing, as well as Daisy, Ethan, John and Lily, who stood nearby. The dog's ears perked up at Cora's voice and he wagged his tail even harder.

"What? Do you think you speak English? Do you understand what I'm saying?" she cooed to the dog, realizing he had a gleam of intelligence and adoration in his eyes. "You are just a big ol' lummox of sweetness, aren't you? Yes, you are!"

"You think you'll be okay with him?" Mike asked tenderly, tucking her hair behind her ear from where it had fallen forward, blocking her view of him. "Dino will be a commitment and if you aren't sure or worried about him…"

"No," Cora interrupted, scrunching up her lips and making kissy faces at the golden retriever mix before her. "You remind me of Mikey, don't you? You're just a softie that wants to be loved all the time. Oh no, you are coming home with me, Mr. Dino," she crooned lovingly and smiled up at Mike.

"I love you so much," she admitted boldly in front of the others, seeing his wide smile. "I adore the fact that you seem to just 'get' me, Mike. Dino is perfect."

"I'm glad you said you loved me," he teased, kissing her at the temple. "I was starting to worry that Dino was going to replace me. I've never seen you make little kisses like that towards me."

"You don't flop down on the ground at my feet when I walk in the room."

"Cora, don't you know that I adore the ground you walk on?"

"Then maybe you should show your belly a little more?" she quipped and instantly heard John smarting off towards Mike playfully.

"Good gravy, no! Have you seen the glare off his skin? The man has the same *'farmer tan'* the rest of us developed in Afghanistan. Trust me, if the sight of Mike's bare stomach doesn't blind you, the reflection of light off of it certainly would."

"Let's not get mean now, ol' man," Mike teased lightly, winking at John. "You are just jealous of my six pack."

"Six pack? Obviously you can't count."

"I wasn't going to brag about how beautiful my rock-hard abs are but if you want me to... I'd be happy to impress all of you here." Mike got to his feet and everyone started laughing. Cora was certain he was about to yank off his shirt and show his stomach. Mike was goofy as could be sometimes and this was just the sort of crazy antic she could picture from him.

She shielded her eyes bashfully but instead Mike dropped right into view on the floor in front of her right next to where Dino lay gazing up at her adoringly. Mike looked at her expectantly and stuck his tongue out to the side, practically mimicking the dog. Cora burst out laughing at the sight of them practically parallel and in the exact same pose.

"Do I get my belly rubbed?"

Mischievously, she reached forward and tickled him only to have him begin laughing uproariously as he tried to get away. Mike pulled at her hands and rolled Cora underneath him. Dino barked loudly nearby before shoving his nose between their faces. They stared at each other; both of their faces alit with sheer happiness in this very moment.

"I love you," they said at the same time and grinned. Cora knew in that very moment that she'd discovered the other half of her soul. Mike was everything she'd wanted and nothing she could have ever expected.

How was she ever going to say goodbye to him?

CHAPTER 10

*C*ora wore sweatpants and a t-shirt to the church that morning so they could get ready together. Her dress had already been staged the night before, as well as her shoes and makeup. Today Ava and Colin would be getting married and it also signified that Mike had just over two weeks in town. He had to fly out on Christmas Eve in order to be able to return in time. Post adjusted his flight in order to be able to travel with Mike, making her feel a little better. He wouldn't be alone and that was some comfort to her, if nothing else.

Hours later, her hair was curled and pulled back with a comb, creating a cascade of curls down the back of her neck that fell just below her shoulders. Her rose colored dress fit perfectly, and she couldn't help but smile as the women put the finishing touches on Ava.

Her dress was stunning in its simplicity. It looked like something Grace Kelly would wear. White satin with no embellishments, fitted at the waist with a flared skirt, and just off the shoulder. She slipped a pair of tiny satin gloves onto her hands as Lily pinned a tiny veil into place on top of her head. It barely came down to her nose but seemed to fit the retro bridal outfit that she wore.

Daisy was sitting on a bench nearby and feeding Aurora a bottle before the ceremony started. Hearing a knock at the door, Cora and Daisy looked at each other curiously.

"I'll get it," Cora said and waved at Ava's panicked expression. "If its Colin – I won't let him in. Don't worry." As she opened the doorway, she saw Mike standing there looking antsy.

"Mike? Is everything okay?"

"Yeah. It's actually pretty great," he admitted awkwardly and then smiled at her. "You look stunning. Do you have a second to talk?" Cora slipped out of the room and shut the door behind her.

"What's going on?"

"Nothing."

"You look like you had a bad meal or something – are you okay?"

"I'm perfect now that I've seen you. Here," he said in a high-pitched voice and grinned. Cora looked down at her hand where he'd crammed something into her palm. It was a small box.

"What is that?" she gaped and stared at him.

"It's a little something to match your dress. Put them on for me, we are fixing to start. I love you," Mike uttered in a rush, grabbing her on the shoulders and kissing her on the cheek. "Gotta go, sweetheart. I'll see you in a few."

Cora stood there staring at him as he took off, practically running back down the hallway of offices to the side of the church building. Standing there, she gingerly pried open the box like it contained something dangerous or venomous. Inside was a pair of pearl earrings that had a slightly pink tinge of color to them.

She glanced up the hallway to see if he was peeking

around the corner watching her reaction because she knew that would be something he'd do. She was utterly alone and could hear the women talking behind the closed door that was to her back. Pulling the earrings from the package, she slipped them on and felt her eyes mist with emotion barely held in check. He was so utterly wonderful and had brought so much to her life in such a short time frame.

"Cora? Is everything okay?"

"Yes – Mike had something for me."

"Oh okay," Lily said, smiling as she tugged on her ear knowingly, "A little something *special*?"

"You knew?"

"Maybe," she admitted. "John just texted, they are heading up the aisle now. Ava is ready to go."

"Sounds good," Cora nodded, following the women down the hallway and waiting at the doorway. As they lined up at the entrance of the chapel, she smiled up at Mike as she put her hand on his arm. "You're the best, you know that?"

"That's funny – I was thinking the same thing about you," he chided gently, teasing her. "You look beautiful."

"You didn't have to get these for me."

"My beautiful girl should always get pretty little things."

"It's extravagant."

"It's your turn, lovebirds – Go!" Daisy interrupted, as Ethan tapped Mike on the shoulder. Startled, Mike and Cora glanced at each other and immediately started down the aisle, parting when they reached the end. Mike went to stand near Colin and was quickly joined by Jamie, John and Ethan.

Cora lined up on the opposite side, followed by Lily and Daisy – who carried Aurora on her hip. Ava joined Colin's side in a breathtaking display of emotion between the two. Both had tears of joy in their eyes and the love they felt for each other was evident to see. Colin broke down during their vows, his voice cracking.

She couldn't help feeling emotional at being able to be a part of this event they were sharing. Glancing at Mike, she saw him watching her, that upturned smile that told her he knew just what she was feeling or thinking. She nodded in acknowledgement and wiped her eyes carefully as to not smudge her mascara. The small ceremony was over in no time it seemed and everyone stepped out into the reception hall attached to the chapel. It was a tiny event with only about twenty to thirty people in attendance – mostly family and coworkers that Ava knew.

"Cora, are you ready to boogie?" Mike asked playfully, pulling her down the hallway towards the reception area. She could hear the loud music from the seventies and eighties playing in the background. He turned around and untied his tie, letting it dangle around his collar on his dress uniform, coaxing her towards the dancefloor where several people were gathering.

In that very moment that she was about to say 'no' to the dancing, she heard the lilting strains of ABBA's 'Dancing Queen' begin to play. She always loved that song growing up. Sighing happily, like it was a sign to her to let loose and enjoy herself – she clapped her hand into his as Mike began to sing to her. Laughing, she let him spin her around the floor.

"Mike," she cried out a little embarrassed, "People are looking at us."

"I don't care," he grinned. "Let them look. I'm going to dance like an insane man with the woman I love for as long as I can. Look at me, don't look at them – and then it won't bother you."

He began rolling his arms in front of him and trying to bump his hip against hers as if to do a bad rendition of the dance move, the hustle. Bursting out laughing again, she saw John was doing the exact same dance with Lily – who was emphatically swinging her hips with abandon left and right, bumping into John. Ethan and Daisy were dancing off to the corner of the dance floor while Ava was speaking with the D.J.

As the song ended, she swirled out onto the dancefloor with an older man as Colin watched proudly from the side. Cora leaned her head on Mike's shoulder as she sighed heavily, seeing Ava dance with her father. Her own father would never dance with her at her wedding, nor would her mother be there.

"Whatcha thinking, sweetheart?" Mike whispered, leaning down to kiss her brow. "You should be smiling right now."

"I'm just thinking and a little bit of an emotional mess."

"Weddings do that to you?"

"I was thinking that Ava was really lucky to have her parents here with her."

"Ahhh," he said knowingly, "Let's get you some punch while they finish their dance. We can get the next song."

Cora followed him without question over to the long table laden with different finger foods, cookies, the wedding cake, and a massive punch bowl. He put some of the red drink into a plastic clear glass and handed it to her with a little napkin. Pouring himself one, he took her hand and exited the hall without a word. He led her back into the now empty sanctuary and sat down on one of the pews at the back of the church. She could still hear the faint melody playing in the background.

"Let's sit for a minute and talk before we head back in," Mike said, unbuttoning the top button of his shirt and tugging at the collar nervously. "Dang, is it warm in here?"

"Well, you were just dancing like a cat having a seizure?" she teased only to roll her eyes at the mock horror on his face at her words.

"I will have you to know that women like a guy that can cut loose like that."

"Where are all these supposed women?" she bantered quickly.

"I don't really know or care – because they aren't the ones that matter to me anyhow," he said quietly, looking at her from under his eyelashes. "I wanted to talk to you about something I've been thinking about and I don't know how you are going to take it."

"Are you breaking up with me?" she asked suddenly, feeling the punch take a sour turn in her stomach almost immediately. "What did I do?"

"What? No, honey," he balked, looking horrified before his features smoothed out after a second. "I was talking about us maybe getting married."

"Huh?" Cora blurted out stupidly and put her hand on her cheek, feeling her skin. "Am I running a fever now? I think I might be delusional. Feel my face, Mike." His finger brushed her cheek ever so tenderly, making her catch her breath. His dark eyes practically gleamed with unfettered love.

"I'm serious, Cora. I want us to get married before I head back."

"You are leaving soon, Mike. What happens then? I don't want to just marry someone who's suddenly gone from my life?"

"I plan on asking to be reassigned as soon as I can," he admitted. "I've been thinking about this the past several days. We can get married and then I can provide for you – I want to take care of you."

"Why is that?"

"I love you and I want you to know you can always depend on me."

"Except when you aren't here."

"Cora, I am coming home – here – to you," he said firmly, grasping her hand in his. "*You* are my home, my everything, and I can't imagine life without you anymore. I want to make you laugh, smile, and dance like we're in the middle of an earthquake," he grinned as she couldn't help the laugh that escaped her.

"I said seizure," she reminded him. Her heart was pounding with happiness and anticipation at his words.

"As my wife, you would have everything and I know you'd be taken care of if something happened..." Cora immediately held up her hand and put it over his mouth to silence him.

"Don't say that," she whispered in a voice she didn't recognize. "You can't die on me, Michael Cooper. Do you understand that?"

"I don't plan on going anywhere for the next fifty years."

"Good."

"But we have to be real about this too. I have to go back to Afghanistan and if something happens to me, I want you taken care of. I want you to have my benefits, my life insurance, and to know that I trust you with everything I am."

"You don't have to do this."

"Cora – I love you. Do you love me?" he asked simply.

"You know that I do. I love you more than the moon and stars," she admitted softly, smiling up at him. He pulled her hand up to his mouth, kissing her knuckles tenderly.

"Then what's a little slip paper when you already have my soul, darling?" he asked gently, growing serious as he nudged the kneeler down. He took her hands in his as he managed to squeeze down between the pews.

"I obviously didn't think this out very well," he confessed, grinning happily. "I might be stuck."

Cora snorted with laughter at his words, which made him start giggling. He was attempting the craziest proposal she'd ever heard of – and it was memorable, completely perfect, and utterly 'classic Mike'.

"Cora Dillion, ever since you came into my life you have been the center of my world. You rock Candy Crush, make a mean peanut butter and jelly sandwich, and kiss like a girl under the bleachers at a high-school football game," he said playfully.

"MICHAEL!" she snapped, trying to pull her hands from his only to have him tug them up to his face, kissing each palm, as he tried to keep from laughing.

"You interrupted me," he chastised with a smirk and cleared his throat noisily, "As I was saying: you are truly the perfect woman for me. You're the Yin to my Yang, the salt to my pepper, the macaroni to my cheese..."

"Oh, you are cheesy alright," she interrupted again, seeing him frown just before he placed her hands directly on his shirt front over his heart. She sat there feeling his heart beat strong and sure under her fingertips. She knew deep down inside that he would never hurt her or betray her. Everything he did, even down to how he acted, was all an act simply to make her laugh or smile. She loved his crazy antics and how he made her feel special.

"You are my world, my universe, and I want everyone to know that you are mine. Will you marry me?" Mike said reverently and released her hands to yank his dog tags out of his shirt. On the simple shot bead chain, she saw the two metal discs along with a simple tiny gold band.

"This was my mother's," he admitted, pulling it off the chain and setting it down on the pew beside her. Her eyes burned with unshed tears as she heard the emotion in his voice. It wasn't a diamond ring but obviously it was infinitely more precious to him. "We can pick out something nicer for you but I..."

"Stop," Cora blurted out. "This is perfect."

"Will you marry me?"

"Yes."

"Will you see if they've got something to slip me out from between the pews? I think my legs are going numb," he blurted out in utter relief and wiped a tear from his eyes. She saw his hands shook with emotion and knew that he was cracking jokes to keep himself together emotionally. He was such a tender-hearted man – *her* man.

"In sickness and in health, right?" she quipped, feeling tears roll down her cheeks. She couldn't help but feel blessed right now to have him in her life. He was truly the best person she'd ever met and the more she was around him, the more she loved his very essence.

"See you... already know... the words," he said with effort as he managed to extract himself from the pew only to sit right next to her, pulling her into his arms. His lips touched hers for several moments before he broke the kiss as he smiled down at her.

"Cora?"

"Mmm?"

"I've got to move."

"Are your legs still numb?"

"No, but my dog tags are *really* poking me," he admitted, pulling her into a hug as he laughed in her hair. "I can't believe I actually forgot and sat on them. I'll admit – you're beauty distracts me and makes me do stupid things."

"Don't blame this on me," she laughed, "It's about time you got up anyhow. You owe me another dance, wild man."

"I prefer the term *'fiancé'*."

"Honestly? I do too - but *'husband'* has a nice ring to it, don't you think?"

"Just so long as I am yours," he said, getting to his feet.

"You certainly are," she promised.

CHAPTER 11

*T*he next two weeks flew by rapidly at a pace that was terrifying. There was so much to do and time seemed to be against them. They didn't announce their engagement at the wedding or even afterwards. It was almost as if Mike was giving her time to process what she was committing to and he was afraid she might change her mind. Trust and relinquishing control of her life was a huge hurdle for her. Mike seemed to understand that and was trying his best to reassure her everything was going to be alright. She found herself staring at the tiny band on her finger repeatedly throughout the day and thinking about how far they had come in the short time she'd known him.

Every day seemed to be a surprise too, another unexpected thing that he did to remove any possible issues for her. Today was no different. He was waiting at her apartment when she got off work, surprising her as he stood there on the curb with his jacket on. She saw his breath escape in little tendrils of fog from the temperature difference.

"What are you doing here?"

"W-wanted t-to s-see you," he shivered, grinning. "It's a-a l-little c-colder than Afghanistan."

"How long have you been out here?" she gaped, grabbing him by the arm and pulling him up to the front door. She hurriedly unlocked it and ushered him inside first.

"B-bout t-twenty m-minutes."

"Are you kidding? Wait," she said suddenly. "Don't take off your jacket. Let me get you some hot tea. Sit down."

Cora urged him to take a seat in the worn-out recliner and draped a crochet afghan over him. Dino immediately jumped onto Mike's lap as if the dog knew he was chilled. Dino had a really bad habit of appearing in her lap when she was alone in the evening. She didn't mind it at all, but unfortunately the sixty-pound dog thought he was barely over ten pounds in his mind. She loved having him around and his loud bark was a comfort as it alerted her when someone was nearby. Hearing the microwave beep, she ran over to drop teabag in the hot water as Dino began to bark several times, causing her to glance up questioningly as someone knocked on the front door.

"S-surprise," he stammered sheepishly, getting to his feet.

"What did you do?"

"H-have I told you I l-love you today?"

Cora smirked at his earnest expression and opened the door a crack, peeking outside. John, Lily, Ethan, Colin, Ava, and Daisy were all crowded on the front stoop of her apartment wearing cheap Santa hats.

"Merry Christmas!" they shouted in unison.

"What is this?"

"We are celebrating early so we can all be together," John said, grinning. His weathered face crinkled at the edges of his eyes. Cora saw that they each held a bowl and had gift bags looped over their wrists.

"Are they here?" Mike asked from behind Cora.

"Who?"

"They were right behind us," John said, not answering her question as he looked at Mike over her shoulder and nodded.

"Okay – let's get busy."

"With what?"

"How attached are you to this chair?"

"It's mine," she sputtered in surprise, "Why?"

"I need to make room."

"For what?"

"My present," he said evasively as everyone filed in the house. They were all smiling and immediately started taking over the place. The breakfast bar for her tiny kitchenette was immediately laden with the covered dishes. Lily picked up the leash that hung on a hook on the wall and hooked it on Dino's collar.

"I'll be right back while you get started," she said in a sing-song voice and headed out the front door. Daisy picked up Aurora out of her carrier and set her on her hip as Mike and John picked up her recliner and carried it out of the apartment. Stunned, she saw Colin and Ethan were picking up her twin-sized mattress and box-spring in the corner.

"What is going on?"

"Cora," Mike said, taking her by the hand and walking her outside. "I mean to take care of my soon-to-be wife and part of that is making sure you don't need a thing. We are also going to have Christmas with everyone, so we needed a place to sit. I thought I would combine the two and surprise you. I hope you aren't mad?"

"Mike, is that…"

"I bought you a desk, baby," he said tenderly, taking his jacket off and putting it on her shoulders. He wrapped his arms around her and rested his head near hers. "I also got a couch so we can sit together with our friends and a bed for when I come home… *Oomph!*"

Cora elbowed him lightly in the midsection. He let go and she turned to look at him. His dark eyes were full of doubt. "Are you mad?"

"Not at all - but I can't do this if you are holding onto me," she said, launching herself into his arms. She was so grateful that he was such a thoughtful and considerate man. Mike picked her up and spun her around slowly, kissing her tenderly.

"That's enough you two," Colin called out, "Cora, can you unhook your computer so we can use the table?"

"What? Oh yes! Don't touch, Bessie," she announced, racing into the house to preserve her ancient computer. Within minutes, she had the computer taken apart and they were moving the table across the emptied room. A large couch was brought in, along with a desk and hutch, and a full-size bed with frame.

Daisy walked over and dropped a large plastic bag on top of the bed, pulling out the contents. Inside were sheets and a comforter. Mike had thought of everything apparently, and it was a little overwhelming to have someone simply take over. She'd never had anyone bring her stuff; it was always taken away in the past, making her feel so very special to know that this was just another way he was taking care of his girl.

The delivery crew finished up and Mike signed the invoice. Ava darted back inside with Dino now that he was out from underfoot. He went immediately to his bowl, ignoring the new items, and began to drink like there was nothing noticeable around him.

"I don't know what to say," Cora breathed, still stunned by the thoughtfulness and planning that had to have gone into this.

"Let's eat!" Colin and Ethan said at the same time, causing everyone to smile and chuckle. The two men were tall and seemed to always have room for food in their stomachs. The lids were removed from the bowls to reveal pistachio salad, a macaroni salad, a bowl of dressing, and a pan of chicken casserole. The last airtight container contained a small frosted cake dusted with white glittery sugar that glistened. Everything looked utterly amazing.

Cora was glad for the distraction. They were supposed to go to the justice of the peace tomorrow and Mike had to fly out in the evening. He'd purposely postponed their wedding till just before he left. Mike had said he wanted her to be sure of what they were doing.

He was still concerned she might be afraid to trust him and he vowed to keep his word to her. He'd given so much of himself in an effort to show that he meant what he said. She'd been stunned when she checked the mail yesterday to see that a box of checks with both of their names had arrived. He'd taken a cue from her, hyphenating everything, in case she had problems and he was on the other side of the world. She'd seen their names together and felt her heart overflow with love for the man that was trying so hard to win her over.

Her house was full of laughter, love, and friendship – something she'd never dreamed of a month ago and was now something she didn't want to give up. They were all squeezed on the large sofa while a few sat on the two dining room chairs. Mike brought more to her life than she'd ever expected.

"I love you," she said suddenly, smiling at his joyous face. He beamed up at her from where he sat on the floor right beside her. The Santa hat was flopped over, making him look completely precocious and adorable.

Colin was apparently quite a shutterbug as he got out his phone and took photos of everyone together. He carefully propped his phone up and with a timer set, they were able to get one of all of them together including Aurora, who was falling fast asleep from all the activity around her.

About an hour later, everyone began to head out due to it getting late in the day. Cora yawned widely, feeling sleepy from having already worked her shift at the claims office. She was really glad she'd put in for a day off and would be able to spend every second with Mike before he left. He seemed to read her mind as he shut the door behind the last person.

"If you don't like anything, you can exchange any of it," he began.

"Truthfully, it's all perfect – even if it's too much."

"There's one more present," he admitted, grinning.

"That's funny, because I have one too." Cora walked over to the canister set that was on the counter of her small kitchen. She was glad that she hadn't hidden the gift anywhere else or else it might have been discovered. She'd planned to give it to him tomorrow, but this just seemed to be so perfect right now. Mike was retrieving one last bag from the corner of the room where he'd dropped his jacket down easily. Dino let out a large *whuff* from his muzzle and promptly went back to sleep where he lay close by.

"Silly dog," he muttered as he petted Dino's head before rejoining her on the couch. As Cora sat there, she glanced at him curiously, trying to see what he had hidden behind him. She saw his eager, mischievous smile and frowned at him.

"You've already done too much."

"I'm making up for lost time – past and present."

"I'm not ready for you to leave tomorrow."

"Lemme tell you – I'm not ready to go either. I promise, I am coming back as soon as I can to the States."

"I know."

"Let's not think about that right now. Let's just enjoy our

first Christmas together. Which of us is going to go first?" Mike asked.

"You first," she said nervously, knowing that her gift was personal. Mike slid out from behind his back a flat box with a large bow on it. He handed it to her and smiled shyly.

"What did you do?" she asked hesitantly at seeing his expression. Cora pulled away the wrapping paper and stopped, feeling tears well up. She set the box down and immediately covered her face to hide the overwhelming emotions she felt right now. He was truly so good to her and she felt so undeserving right now.

"I love you, sweetheart," he whispered, putting his arms around her and cradling her to his chest.

"You shouldn't have," she cried out tearfully against his shirt. He'd bought her a brand-new laptop for her fledgling business she was trying to build. It was an incredible gift that told her that not only did he listen, he cared, he understood, and wanted to support her. He was truly unbelievable.

"Do you like it?"

"I freakin' love it," she laughed tearfully against his chest where she'd tucked her head. Wiping her eyes, she tenderly kissed him and nodded happily. "This is perfect, and I can't wait to set it up."

"I'm glad."

"But I will do that in a few minutes – it's time for your present."

"You didn't have to get me anything," he said tenderly. "Just having you in my life is enough."

"Stop that or I will cry all night," she warned, smiling tremulously as she pulled a tiny box out from behind her. He looked at her curiously as she handed it to him.

"It's a little something that I saw and needed to get. It just hit me and well…" Cora explained shyly. She didn't want to admit that she'd seen the display and had been completely bowled over. Mike opened the box and didn't move. He sat there frozen with his head bent for several moments making her wonder if she'd made a mistake. When he looked up at her, she knew that her gut instincts had been right on the money. Mike's eyes glistened with unshed tears as he smiled at her.

"I seriously love you woman," he admitted thickly, slipping the matching wedding bands out of the box. He held the smaller of the two up and held out his hand. He took the ring and hesitated before slipping it onto her finger.

"I like the shape. They remind me of little matching crowns. It's kind of fitting because you make me feel like a king when you smile at me."

"Actually, I saw them and realized it was perfect for the prince of my heart," I had them engrave our initials together on the inside of each band," she confessed. She'd taken her computer money that she'd saved and bought the set as soon as she'd seen them.

"With this ring, I thee wed," he said huskily, slipping it onto her finger and kissing it as if to seal it in place. "I will never forget this moment as long as I live. You are my everything, my soulmate, sweet Cora."

She felt almost a sense of relief mingled with joy as she slipped the ring onto his trembling finger. She loved him more than life itself and would wait for him to return until the end of time if need be. He was right – they were everything to each other. There was no Mike without Cora – and no Cora without Mike. With him leaving tomorrow would be like saying goodbye to her very soul. Her world would darken at three fifty in the afternoon when his plane departed.

THEY CUDDLED on the new couch for hours as the Christmas tree glowed from the corner of the small apartment. The faint sounds of his heartbeat under her cheek was so comforting. Neither one of them wanted to part, knowing what was coming. Instead, Cora draped a throw over herself and gave one to Mike as they simply lay there on the couch together. She didn't want to miss a second away from him. At some point, they both fell asleep on the couch.

The sun streaming through the blinds the next morning served to be nature's alarm clock as they woke early. Time seemed to go by so quickly, and before she knew it, they were standing in front of the judge at the courthouse saying their vows. Sliding the ring onto his finger once again, she realized that in her heart she'd married Mike last evening when they'd done this very thing. Smiling up at her new husband, she saw that he was grinning.

"A little *de-ja vu*, sweetheart?"

"Quite a bit."

Jamie had come to witness their wedding since he was also flying out soon. It was as if he could read her thoughts, causing Jamie to glance at Cora sadly.

"Mike, we are going to have to go."

"I know. Cora, are you going to be okay?"

"Is *'no'* an option?"

"You know I don't want to leave my little bride right now."

"I just want you to be safe and come back as soon as you can."

"Nothing could keep me away – part of the reason we waited to do this."

"The honeymoon?"

"Our wedding night," he said tenderly, smiling. "The thought of you being my wife will keep me motivated in

114

finding a way to return to you. The worst case, if they deny me a transfer, I can get out in four years."

"Are you kidding me?"

"I wish I was."

"You could have shared that before you married me," she said painfully and saw him wince. The thought of not seeing him again except for his military leave hurt too much.

"It's not going to be four years," he breathed, pulling her into his arms. "I promise you."

"I'm going to hold you to that."

"You can trust me, sweetheart," he vowed, kissing her tenderly on her brow as Jamie interrupted again.

"I hate being the bad guy – but we really have to go or we might miss our flight."

Cora nodded and pulled away from Mike, her emotions on overload right now. She'd just gone through the greatest high in her life, marrying the man of her dreams, to crashing down to the ultimate low… saying goodbye. She was numb to the very core right now simply to keep from breaking down. They loaded quickly into her car where their large canvas duffle bags were still waiting. When she got to the airport, Jamie put his hand on her shoulder and looked at Mike.

"We've got forty minutes to get through security and to the gate. I'm sorry, Cora," she heard Jamie utter, his words full of regret. "I feel like such a heel right now, but you've got to drop us off here. We gotta go, Mike. Dude – I am really sorry."

Mike uttered an expletive and turned to where Cora sat, clenching the steering wheel. His eyes swung towards her, and she saw the raw pain glimmering in their dark depths.

"Go," she whispered, feeling her heart breaking in two. She knew deep down inside that Mike would miss his flight deliberately if he knew she was hurting. "I'm okay. You are coming home when you can."

"I *swear* it."

"I don't want you to get in trouble."

"I want you to know I will keep my word. I love you so much."

"Mike," she barely got out as he leaned over quickly, kissing her intensely.

"Brakes! Hit the brakes! We're rolling!" Jamie hollered immediately, patting them on the heads to separate the two of them. Cora stomped on the brake pedal and winced as she saw her car was almost touching a huge Tahoe in front of her. Jamie opened the back door and slid out. He then opened Mike's door, and she felt like her fragile front she was putting out was in jeopardy of breaking into a million pieces.

"I love you, little wife," Mike said trying to smile.

"You better hurry home, little husband," she bantered, smirking playfully as she felt her eyes and nose begin to burn from unshed tears. "Jamie, take my husband with you and make sure he makes his flight. I don't want him in trouble."

"Yes, Mrs. Cooper," Jamie said with a somber salute.

"Watch out for him," Cora ordered painfully, nodding. She turned to Mike. "I'll be waiting."

"Yes ma'am."

CHAPTER 12

*M*arch 2017

CORA HEARD Dino's whine deep in his belly as he lay across her lap on the couch while she sat there watching the evening news. Petting the dog, Dino suddenly scrambled to his feet and ran down from the couch, scratching Cora's leg in the meantime. Barking, she felt a shiver of unease run down her spine as the dog stood right in front of the door.

"What's wrong?"

A loud knock made Cora jump fearfully as she slid off the couch and glanced out the door. Rolling her eyes, she realized that she hadn't changed the burnt-out porch bulb just yet and couldn't see who was standing there.

"Who is it?" she asked loudly and projected her voice. "Calm down, Killer – if I open the door, you can't attack like you did last time."

Cora glanced down at the large yellow dog that was staring up at her, wagging his tail happily at the attention.

The dog would lick an intruder to death or trip them when he flopped down on the floor lovingly wanting his belly patted.

"It's your husband."

Yanking open the door, Cora stared at Mike's exhausted face. His eyes were full of love and adoration as he stood there in the shadows. Dino instantly jumped up on him, pushing Cora to the side, his paws nearly reaching Mike's shoulders.

"Did your mama rename you Killer?" Mike teased, petting the dog and smiling at Cora. "Can I come in, little wife?"

"You're home," she breathed happily.

"I had a promise to keep," he smiled, "A promise I intended to keep to the woman I love more than life itself. You are looking at the newest recruiter assigned to desk duty in Tyler."

"Are you serious?"

"As a heart-attack," Mike chuckled, pushing the dog down so he could embrace her. Kissing her tenderly, he smoothed her hair away from her face and looked into her eyes.

"They said I had a gift and could talk my way out of anything."

"You'll be wonderful at the job."

"I don't know," he admitted, "If any of these boys have someone they adore half as much as I love you – I'll never talk them into signing up."

"Oh, I don't know," she chided tenderly, "You can be pretty convincing."

"Does that mean you've fallen in love with me again, my lovely little wife?"

"I've never stopped loving you."

"I think it's time we got caught up on time we've missed while we were apart."

"We do have quite a bit of time to make up for," she

announced tenderly, smoothing his brow as he stared at her lovingly with his dark intense eyes that burned like hot coals.

"How about starting with that wedding night I owe you?" he said huskily, wrapping his arms around her waist. Cora reached over and closed the front door, throwing the lock with an audible click.

"See? You've already got me convinced," she said with a wide smile. "You'll make an incredible recruiter."

AFTERWORD

Thank you for taking the time to read Remember Joy. If you enjoyed it, please consider telling your friends or posting a short review. Doesn't have to be much, just a simple rating and a few kind words work wonders. Your thoughts, opinions and feedback are much appreciated.

Sincerely,

Ginny

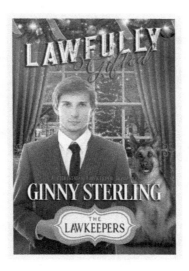

CPO John Griffin's story - the book that launched the series
Healing Hearts

Dear John...

For teacher Lily Hogan, those words would come to mean so much.
She knew that giving back to the community brought joy into
people's lives. When her fourth-grade class writes letters to the
military overseas in Afghanistan, she takes up her own pen and
leads her students by example – writing a letter to an unknown
soldier.

CPO John Griffin and his K-9 dog, Radar, have been through so
much together over the last several years. Sniffing out bombs,
searching the hills and mentoring his team, he feels so alone and
unsure of his future- until a letter reminds him that there's more to
life in this world he's protecting. Simple words, a kind gesture and

feeling that he isn't forgotten out there in the desert, compels him to write back. Before long, he finds himself looking forward to the care packages and letters from his pen-pal halfway across the world.

With every letter and every word, they begin to develop a friendship and wonder what the other person is truly like? Major life changes are scary enough as it is - but is it possible to fall in love with someone before you've even laid eyes upon them? Can the magic of the season bring the sweetest gift of all?

Lucy Reyes didn't need anyone interfering with her life as an investigative reporter. She'd found out the hard way that having to depend on someone made you weak and left you vulnerable. When she overhears a private conversation that leaves her feeling sorry for an unknown soldier, she takes up the mantle and begins writing the stranger who'd been betrayed.

Jamie Post had always known the direction of his life. He had a fiancée back home and was working diligently to be a strong provider until he discovers that Annabelle's loyalty lies elsewhere - in someone else's arms. Jamie takes what comfort he can in purging all his thoughts and emotions to a stranger on the other side of the world, when suddenly Lucy materializes on base in Afghanistan in jeopardy.

Can Lucy tackle a job in the middle of a warzone while fighting the feelings inside of her? Will Jamie discover that letting down his guard means letting someone back into his heart? Can fate intervene, bringing these two hearts together in a world torn apart?

Available for Preorder now

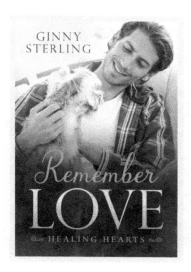

Get your copy of Remember Love

Ava Richardson is a new mother with a child she never expected. When a nightmare event rips her from a fairytale life, she's devastated and frightened to move on. What she never expected was to find solace in a pen-pal, pouring out her feelings to a stranger halfway across the world.

Colin Wilkes is a weary, reckless soldier in Afghanistan. Saddled with guilt at causing his best friend to lose his leg, he awaits whatever fate he has coming. Unexpectedly receiving an email from a strange woman looking for anything to help her get through the day- he can't help but feel intrigued and sympathetic to her pleas.

When Colin finds himself suddenly back in the States and face to face with his mysterious pen-pal, can a friendship that began over the internet solidify into something more? Can one shattered soul help mend another? Can they be saved by remembering just how to love someone?

Grab An Agent for Gillian- Click here!

Two wrongs don't make a right – or do they?

Gillian Jameson had lost her world when her husband died. Alone, scared, and desperate for something to fill the emptiness in her soul- she turns to the Pinkerton Agency for help. What she never expected was to be married again, especially to a man like Cade Malone.

Cade had a recklessness to him that was born of sheer desperation. His wife and child were gone. He was running from memories that haunted him with every breath and nightmares that plagued him each night. What he needed was a reason to go on- and it certainly wasn't in the form of a new partner.

Can two broken souls form a bond between them? Will seeing

another person who is struggling to deal with the trauma in their lives be just the thing to help old wounds heal – or would falling for each other simply create another emotional scar that is just too great to bear?

ABOUT THE AUTHOR

Ginny Sterling is a Texas transplant living in Kentucky. She spends her free time (Ha!) writing, quilting, and spending time with her husband and two children. Ginny can be reached on Facebook, Instagram, Twitter or via email at GinnySterlingBooks@gmail.com

Subscribe now to my Newsletter for updates